Apache Country

When part-time cavalry scout Murphy agrees to ride out and warn the Arizona settlers that Apaches have jumped the reservation, all he expects is a bunch of dedicated killer Indians after his scalp. But when he runs into Rosemary, a beautiful woman with a voice as big as all outdoors, he finds himself pitted against ruthless enemies of every kind including kidnappers, comancheros and renegade Apaches.

But most implacable of all, there is the Sonoran Desert itself, where everything that grows either bites, stings or scratches.

Murphy needs all his skill with a gun if he is to survive.

Apache Country

WALT MASTERSON

Dorset County Library

203867353

Askews   2002

£10.50

A Black Horse Western

ROBERT HALE · LONDON

© Walt Masterson 2002
First published in Great Britain 2002

ISBN 0 7090 7103 5

Robert Hale Limited
Clerkenwell House
Clerkenwell Green
London EC1R 0HT

The right of Walt Masterson to be identified as
author of this work has been asserted by him
in accordance with the Copyright, Designs and
Patents Act 1988.

Typeset by
Derek Doyle & Associates, Liverpool.
Printed and bound in Great Britain by
Antony Rowe Limited, Wiltshire.

For Walt Zagorsky, the only man I know who really did carry a gun on the streets of Tombstone, Arizona

ONE

At the edge of the dry wash, a pebble ran down the bank and provoked a tiny avalanche of dust which slid silently after it. Murphy tightened his hand on the mustang's nostrils. If he had dared make a sound, he would have cursed. He should never have left the Indians out of his calculations, but a man gets careless sometimes, and this was one of those times.

His ear, pressed against the ground, could hear the ponies pacing along the trail above the wash. There were at least ten Apache in the group, and by rights they should have been way over in the Dragoons at this time.

The mustang was getting restless; he felt it try to raise its head and slid over its neck to hold it down. The dun–coloured horse was a stayer, a horse with speed and bottom, but it had never had much in the way of brains, and there was a limit to the amount of time any horse would stay grounded while other horses were walking nearby. It wanted to call to them, to go and see them, to socialize.

Apache Country

The Apache would be glad to socialize, too. But their socializing would involve slow fires, or ants' nests, or rawhide and sun. Murphy eased the Smith & Wesson into his hand, and did his best not to make a sound.

By now, the Indians had passed his position behind the desert sumac at the bottom of the wash, and would have to look back to see him. It didn't mean he was safe, but it did give him an edge. He laid more of his weight on the horse's neck.

He cursed the war; he cursed the military men back East who had stripped the western garrisons to fight the war, and left the civilian settlers exposed to the Apache; he cursed the man who had burned the old Fort Burnside, and he cursed himself for volunteering.

'Never volunteer,' his father had told him. 'You don't have to volunteer to get yourself killed. Some bastard officer will do it for you, every time.'

Now it looked as though Lieutenant Bassenger had managed to get Murphy killed, though Murphy had to admit he had co-operated with the fool pretty damn' enthusiastically. Trouble was, he just wanted to get out of the fort at the top of Apache Pass and down into the desert.

Also, he had been worried about the Woolgars. Old man Woolgar had been the first to offer help when Murphy had been down on his luck, and now was pay-back time. Murphy just wanted to gather up the old man, Newt, his useless, spineless son-in-law and Mandy, his pretty, buxom daughter and get them somewhere with more soldiers than Indians

Apache Country

and a wall around it.

The horses' hoofbeats had faded now, which meant they were out of sight along the wash, and he allowed the tawny horse to get to its feet, though he held grimly onto its nostrils. A high whinny would carry over the desert flatness like a trumpet call.

He slipped the Smith & Wesson back into its holster, and remounted the animal. In this period, the desert was not at its hottest, but the heat sucked the water out of a man, and his mouth was dry and uncomfortable. He found himself a pebble and popped it into his mouth to stimulate salivation, but it was a deception at best, and he knew it.

The Woolgar ranch was several miles to the north of him, in the elbow of the only river in this part of the Sonoran Desert which would be likely to carry water at any time of year. He had watered last at Apache Springs, in the little green fold of ground just under the guns of the fort, and he needed water badly. He shook his canteen and listened to the pitiful slosh of the very little water within, then wet his bandanna and wiped out the horse's nostrils and mouth. It whickered softly and after taking a swig of water himself, he poured the rest into the crown of his hat and let the horse finish it.

There was water up in the Dragoons, if you knew where to look for it, and there was a well at Tubac, even if the garrison there had been withdrawn. Or, of course, there was Tumacacori.

Twenty years ago, Tubac had been the biggest town in this part of the Arizona Territory, but when the soldiers went, the Apache came, and a wise man

Apache Country

did not hang around when there were Apaches on their way.

Tumacacori on the other hand was a church built like a fortress. Once he had collected the Woolgars, he could take them down there and find Lieutenant Bassenger and the patrol to bring them back into Fort Bowie or over to Tucson.

Bowie, these days, was a real fort. Water nearby, stone walls, artillery pieces to clear the hills, a full garrison.

He pressed on north and west, with the sun in his face, now, and his back to the way the Indians had been going.

They were on their way south to the border, he thought. The group which had passed him were carrying heavy from the look of their horses' hoofprints, beaten deeply into the soft sand along the top of the wash. Either a successful hunting party carrying meat, a group of refugees from the San Carlos making their way down to join Geronimo, or returning from a successful raid carrying loot.

To an Apache, loot was just a few things: women, horses, weapons, or food. They had little use for manufactured goods unless they were made of metal. Needles, buckles, fish hooks – Murphy flashed his teeth in a mirthless grin at the idea of an Apache using fish hooks – buttons. All things the Apache could not make for himself and all of them things which would draw the Indian closer into dependence on the white invaders of his land.

Murphy topped out, careful not to skyline himself

Apache Country

on the low ridge, and drew the binoculars from his saddle-bag. Out there to the south, towards the line of long, low hills which marked the border, there was the suggestion of dust in the desert air. If he had been looking towards the sun, he would not have seen it, but against the darker mountains, it was there, misty but unmistakable. Dust, raised by a group of men travelling slowly and carefully. The Apache party he had just passed.

The Woolgar ranch was away to his north-west still, and he swung the binoculars that way. No signs of life, but then he had not expected any. There did seem, though, to be a smudge which could be smoke.

He put the glasses away again and urged the horse down the hill and towards the ranch on the San Pedro.

Behind him, a good long way back, an Apache warrior swung from his pony and examined the ground. Here, a stone had been turned over in the shade of a saguaro, and the faintly darker stain on its underside had not yet dried out. The stone had been upset in the last hour, or the dry heat of the desert would have dried it completely. Further on, the Apache found the broken stem of a desert juniper. There was a pair of light, dun hairs caught in the stem, where a horse's shoulder had pushed against it.

He hopped back onto his pony, and loaded one of his precious bullets into the cavalry carbine. If he was right, and the rider up to the north was a white man, there would be more guns – maybe even a repeater rifle and certainly a shoots-six in a gunbelt, maybe full of bullets. And a horse, of course.

Suddenly, it seemed like a good day to the Apache. He urged the pony into a quick-pacing walk, keeping a sharp eye open for the tracks of the man he hurried to kill.

Murphy had heard a preacher once describe the desert as a place of unbroken sand and rock, and shaken his head in wonder that such a well-educated man could be so wrong. The Sonoran Desert stretched out around him, green and brown, and far away at the furthest extent of his vision the next ridge of mountains waited, dark purple in the sun. Admittedly the green which covered the desert was the green of cactus, and virtually every plant he could see was guaranteed to either spike him, sting him or scratch him, but it was a plant.

He saw the low-lying smoke halfway across the flat, and he cursed long and low when he did see it.

The Woolgar ranch was about there.

He topped out on a low rise, south of the ranch, and swung down from the horse to avoid skylining himself again, putting the binoculars to his eyes. Below him, and a little to the north, was the Oak Creek ranch house.

The base of the column of smoke, sure enough, came from the blackened remains of the ranch building. The corrals were broken down, and he could see the burned-out remains of the family's wagon. Near the wagon, a bright bit of cloth fluttered fitfully in the wind.

Meanwhile, to the south, from which direction he

Apache Country

had just come, there was a suggestion of more dust.

Murphy suppressed the temptation to race down to the ranch. The war party he had passed may well have been the same warriors who had raided the ranch, but equally, they may not.

Murphy had been a trapper, shot buffalo for the army, fought in the Civil War, soldiered abroad and tracked for virtually every horse soldier commander the government had ever sent West. He was a believer in listening to his instincts, and his instinct told him that back there was an Apache brave with murder in his heart and a rifle in his hand, heading straight for Murphy. The fact that he was moving fast meant he was either young and inexperienced, or very confident. Certainly he was a fine tracker if he could follow Murphy's carefully obscured trail at anything more than a crawl. Murphy did not believe in careless Indians, so he had to assume the one trailing him was simply very confident.

He climbed onto his horse again, and moved on towards the ranch.

At the water, he dismounted and filled his canteen, letting the horse drink sparingly.

There was still dust in the air to the south as he made his way along the far bank of the river, and he kept a wary eye on it. He knew the Apache would come to him now, and it was merely a case of picking his ground for the meeting.

Halfway there, he found what he was looking for. The tracks of several horses had come down from the ranch, and waited by the creek, then continued

Apache Country

to the south. They had been watering their horses.

He rode on, making no attempt to conceal himself or his approach, to the ruins of the ranch and the ruins of his friends.

TWO

The Apache could see that the man ahead was making for the smoke of the burning ranch. He came to the top of the hill, and read the signs that the rider had paused there and surveyed the land ahead.

He had been aware of the war party which had left the San Carlos to go south to join Geronimo in Mexico, but he had been too late to join it, so he made his own way south. His alternative was Natche, who was also out of the reservation.

He was, like the rest of his people, sick to his very soul of army beef at short weight, of the restrictions of the reservation, of the contempt with which he and his people were treated by the agent.

The way he had got his carbine had been pure luck. The soldier had been alone, watering the horses within sight of the fort, but he had been careless.

He wanted to light his pipe.

As he sucked on the first mouthful of smoke, his carbine slipped on the rock and clattered to the

Apache Country

ground. The soldier, still sucking, bent to pick it up, and felt, with a start of alarm, that his hat had been removed.

His dying lungs expelled the smoke in one long plume, which the Apache found almost beautiful. He had never actually seen a man's dying breath before, and he watched with pleasure as it dissipated on the evening air, white against the dark of the rocks.

He put down the rock with which he had dashed out the young soldier's brains, slipped his cartridge pouch and belt off the body, and took the carbine. Then he chose the best horse from the picket line, threw his blanket over it and used the lead rein as a harness.

The rest of the horses simply went on watering. The Apache would have liked to steal them, also, but he knew the departure of all the horses would be seen immediately, and they would raise dust.

By the time the sergeant had noticed that his trooper was missing, and sent a guard piquet to find out where he was, the Apache was several miles away, and travelling fast.

Now, he looked forward to having a second horse, and more guns. He approached the ranch house with great caution. He left his horse in a grove of cottonwoods along the creek, let himself down into the water, and crawled down in the shadow of the bank until he was opposite the yard of the ranch and the smoking, remaining standing parts of the building.

Smoke trickled out of the embers and he could smell burned flesh.

Apache Country

Upstream, nothing. Bare earth, a couple of cholla, some sagebrush. Nothing big enough to conceal a man, certainly not a white man.

With infinite caution, he raised himself from the stream bed, his attention focused on the prickly pear and the rocks downstream.

Crouching, he ran out of the stream bed towards the rocks. There was a faint rustle of movement over to his right, upstream, and he spun towards it.

Murphy, rising from the empty desert like a corpse from the grave, shot him twice through the chest. Both bullets went through the silver hoop which hung from his neck on a turquoise and silver necklace, and shattered his heart.

Murphy stepped forward to examine his kill. The warrior, as he had suspected, was a Chiricahua Apache, barrel-chested, flat-faced and thin.

Murphy stripped the cavalry belt and bullet pouch off him, and picked up the carbine. The man's knife, a long, bright finger of steel, he tucked into the top of his boot.

He walked down the creek until he found the Indian's horse, and led it back to the ranch, tethering it where it could get at the water.

Then, because he could no longer postpone the task, he went to work with a spade. He dug the grave deep and wide, because it had to contain four.

He put Newt and Mandy together at one end of the grave, since they had at least died together. From the empty cartridge cases at the scene of their last stand at the barn, Newt had not been quite such a pathetic character after all. He must have held out

Apache Country

for some time, and he had put his last cartridge into his wife's head.

He had been stabbed in the eye, and his body had been thoroughly mutilated, though which came first, Murphy could not tell.

Mandy had been pregnant at her death, and Murphy laid the body of the tiny boy in the grave with his parents.

Old man Woolgar had been a different matter. From the look of it, he had simply run out of ammunition without taking the precaution of saving his last round for himself. Him, they had hung head down over his own wagon wheel and set the vehicle on fire.

Whether he had survived long enough to watch them destroy his house and all he had built up over years of back-breaking labour and a surprisingly good relationship with the Apache, it was impossible to tell. He had died hard, anyway.

Murphy was not a forgiving man, so he did not bury the Apache.

'The coyotes got a right to live, too,' he muttered.

Then he said over the mass grave the words he could remember of the burial service, which he had attended more times than he liked to recall, and left the dead to their sleep.

He rode away towards the mountains which stood between him and Tumacacori, leading the Apache's stolen horse. The animal proclaimed its origin with the US brand on its hip, and seemed glad to be going with someone who smelled familiar.

The desert sunset painted the western sky red

ahead of him, and he would have to hole up and sleep somewhere out in the sagebrush, but nothing on earth would have tempted him to spread his blankets in the cottonwoods near the smell of the burning ranch house. The Navajo, he knew, believed the spirits of the unhappy dead remained in the buildings where they died, and what was good enough for the Navajo was good enough for Murphy. He liked the Navajo.

Just at that moment, he liked almost everybody better than the Apache.

Rosemary Dodd walked alongside the family wagon in the heat of the morning, keeping her eye open for dry wood and kindling. There had been cactus skeletons and twigs easily gathered when they started south from Tucson, but now, on the third day, they seemed to have been cleared by someone else.

She knew they needed fire tonight if they were going to eat, and with three extra mouths to feed, she would need a big fire.

The thought made her glance sideways at the man riding at the head of the horses. Not welcome mouths, either, she reminded herself. She did not like any of the people who had joined up with them just outside Tucson.

Three men in travel-stained clothes, they had simply cantered up and announced that they were going to accompany the wagons south.

'Be a bit o'extra safety for you, and a bit o' comp'ny fer us, I reckon,' said the leader of the three.

Apache Country

He had winked at Rosemary when he said it, and she didn't like the wink.

She might be a servant, but she was not his servant. There were a few things about him and his friends that she noticed, too. Their clothes might be travel-stained and worn but their weapons were clean and well tended. Each man had a Colt holstered at his hip, the holster tied down, and a Winchester in his saddle boot. Each had at least one more pistol tucked into his belt, and their Bowie knives were more like short swords.

Then there was the matter of their horses. Most horses ridden by working men in Arizona were tough, hard-working cow ponies, but these three rode blood stock. There was Arab in the tight-drawn, pointed muzzles of these horses, and Arab blood cost a lot of money. These three men did not look as if they had two cents to scratch their backsides with.

'Mighty fine grub, ma'am,' said the dark one called Cisco. He was marginally better than either red-haired, thickset Brennan or Darker, their leader. Darker had gone out of his way to be amiable when the three had first rode in, but his mask of joviality had slipped every now and again, and he became more familiar the further they got from civilization.

She smiled to herself when she realized that she meant Tucson. The little town strung along the bank of the Rillito in the shadow of the Santa Catalinas would have horrified her at one time, with its primitive conditions, its swaggering toughs and its heat and smell. Now she thought of it as

Apache Country

civilization. The more so since it also contained soldiers.

Civilization, she thought, was all relative. When her father died, and the Davey family had offered her a job, cooking and cleaning for them, as well as teaching at the school, she was grateful enough. When they announced they were moving West, she even welcomed the idea as a new beginning.

But when they decided to leave the wagon train and head south for Mexico, where Japhet heard there were silver mines, her heart sank.

When they started West, he was going to be a farmer, but on a grand scale. Then he heard about the price the army would pay for beef and horses, so the farm he was going to build became a ranch. Exactly where he was going to raise the coin to buy a herd, she had no idea, for the family had plunged all its capital into the wagons and stock to bring them out to the frontier. Then he heard of the Mexican silver mines, and saw himself as a prospector. Rosemary viewed this ambition with alarm. But she had no money to invest, and if her employer was going south, she had no choice but to go with him.

She liked the Daveys: Japhet might be a dreamer, but he was also an amiable, honest man willing to do a good day's work.

He was, she knew, running away from failure in the hope of catching up with success. Plenty of men had walked and worked their way to a good new life in the West.

For herself, she would look out for a business opportunity wherever they settled down. She was a

Apache Country

good cook and not afraid of hard work. Western men liked their vittles, and she could provide them with the finest. Put her down in a kitchen in a Western town, she reckoned, and she would have them riding in from miles around to eat her cooking.

But Mexico was something else again.

Her arms were full, and she walked back to the wagon to throw the fuel into the net stretched underneath it. Half full already, so they had enough fuel for their cooking fire, and to keep them warm through the cold desert night.

She got herself a drink from the water barrel, being careful to turn off the tap and tie it back with a thong to prevent the jolting of the wagon from knocking it loose. Water was life here, and the body seemed to soak up every drop and beg for more.

A shadow fell across her as she swung away from the wagon, and she looked up into Darker's face. The big man and his horse had approached without her hearing them, and the closeness of the animal gave her a shock.

'You startled me,' she said, squinting up at him, dazzled by the brightness of the afternoon sky.

He grinned, suddenly. His smile lit up what was a brooding, heavy face, and some of the menace went out of it.

'You'll get used to me,' he said. 'I ain't so bad. Once you get to know me good.'

She heard Cisco chuckle, and knew there was a joke in there somewhere. She did not want to know exactly what it was, and she did not like being the subject of a joke.

Apache Country

Darker swung his horse away, and stood in the stirrups to peer towards the West. She could see a range of low hills over there and the misty tops of some cottonwoods.

The day before, they had passed the old Spanish mission of San Xavier del Bac and watered their stock at the fathers' well. As soon as they left the mission, Darker had swung the wagons away towards the east, where taller, craggier mountains reared.

'Santa Ritas,' he told her, waving at them. 'Water down there, two days' time.' But there would be water where the cottonwoods were, she knew. Why were they pulling away from them, out into the desert towards the mountains, where the going would be much harder?

Next time she brought wood back to the wagon, she climbed over the tailboard and dived into her bedroll. Tucked away out of sight there she kept the short-barrelled Colt her father wore when he was a law officer. She checked the loads, pulled up her skirts and belted the weapon so that it hung in front of her where the dress bunched round her hips. It might make her look a mite bulkier, she reckoned, but with its butt under the waistband where she could get at it, she felt safer.

Rosemary was well aware that she was a big woman. All her life she had been taller, broader and deeper bosomed than other women. Men, she knew, valued a slender waist and slim hips, but she got her share of attention. She might never be fashionable, but when she put her mind to it, she could be magnificent, and she knew it.

Apache Country

Just at the moment, though, she was not trying to stop a show. She was trying to persuade herself that her suspicions were unfounded.

She climbed over the wagon load, and dropped onto the seat beside Babs Davey. Japhet's wife was everything Rosemary was not: slender, blonde, cool and fresh-faced. She did not suit the desert, and the desert returned the compliment. It made her face turn brick red, and dried her out. She hated the heat and distrusted everything that grew or crawled in it. But she was a farmer's wife; she could handle stock and she could drive a wagon. With Japhet driving the rear one and Babs the lead wagon, the little party was making good time. Her children, Rory and Meg, helped Rosemary with the chores, and they were a happy enough party.

'Hi, Rosemary,' said Babs without looking round. 'Need a rest?'

Rosemary shook her head.

'A look at the compass,' she said under her breath, then, 'I certainly do. It's hotter than a fry-pan out there!'

She said it loud for Cisco's benefit, because the rider had glanced back at her, and she waited until his horse stumbled and took his attention before she reached under the seat and pulled out the boxed compass.

A quick look at it sufficed and she closed the case and slipped it into its locker in the seat. Then she sat back with her heart pounding.

They were headed due east, into the Sonoran Desert, instead of south to Mexico.

Apache Country

She had talked to men and women in Tucson, and she knew that if they wanted to get to Mexico, they needed to head due south. East lay only the desert, and the ruins of the worked-out mines. Yet Darker had headed them quite deliberately out there.

Why? She had a dreadful idea she knew the answer.

'Babs,' she said, quietly, 'have you got a gun?'

Babs threw a frightened look at her.

'Gun?' she said. 'No. Why?'

Cisco was dropping back, and Rosemary got up to climb off the wagon box.

'Get one,' she had time to say, before the man was riding beside them.

She started to drop to the ground, but Cisco caught her round the waist, and set her down. His hand was unnecessarily high on her body, but she ignored the insult because she was glad it had not gone low enough to feel the butt of her pistol.

THREE

Murphy urged the horse up the slope of a low ridge, pulled off his hat and stopped the horse when his eyes were just clear of the skyline. He had checked three ranches after leaving the Woolgar place, and found the families missing from all three. A note on the kitchen table of one said simply: SODJERS COM TO GET US. GON TO TOOSON. EAT. SLEEP. LEAVE PLACE CLEEN. MA GENTRY.

He had eaten and slept, rested the horses in the corral, and moved on. Another scout must have come down from Tucson to clear out these families, so his mission was all but over. He had also cleaned up after himself, washed the plates in the creek and racked them in the kitchen. Ma Gentry was a house-proud woman whose words were not to be ignored. Not if he wanted doughnuts with his coffee next time he called by here, and Murphy was a man who dearly loved a plate of sweet, sugary doughnuts.

He liked the Gentrys. Ma was a regular gorgon, built like a bear with a temper to match and a tongue like a crosscut saw. But George, her big

Apache Country

Dutch husband, had an easy laugh and a satisfied, contented look about him which said he was a happily married man.

They had seven sons, too, which had to say something about their marriage. The boys all took after their father, big and beefy with easy-going ways and loud laughs. Come to think about it, the loudest noise in their noisy home was the laughter.

The only thing they disagreed about was the Apaches. Murphy made no secret of the fact that he sympathized with the Indians. If someone had come along and settled down to drive Murphy out of his home, murdered his children and enslaved his wife, Murphy would have behaved exactly as the Indians had.

However, he also thought that the westward tide would not be stemmed, and however much he sympathized with the plight of the Apache, it would not help him if he found himself one day hanging head down over a slow fire.

He swung the horses suddenly behind a clump of rocks and shrub and cursed under his breath. Ahead of him, riding for the pass between the Sycamores and the Santa Ritas, was a line of horsemen. They were not cavalry, and certainly not miners, so they were Indians.

For him to attempt to follow them through, or to sneak past them in the night would be foolhardy and, as Murphy was fond of pointing out, Mrs Murphy didn't have no foolish children.

Well, matter of fact, she had, he admitted to

Apache Country

himself. Foolish, like volunteering to go out and bring in the ranchers when he was asked, even though he was a scout and not a soldier, any more. Foolish, like getting himself swung in behind a bunch of Apaches on their way to....

On their way to what, exactly? he wondered, suddenly. There was water down on the flanks of the Sycamores, sure, but they would not need it unless they were aiming for something down there, or on the trail between Tucson and the border, away to the south.

He sat still until the dust had settled in the wake of the Apaches and then waited five more minutes to make sure there were no stragglers lagging behind, then he rode down the hill and turned his horse's head up into the Santa Ritas.

There was water over the other side of the mountains, and here a man went from water to water. There was a ghost trail over the top of the mountains, and then he could drop down to Tubac and Tumacacori. He would water at the springs, and then move south. If there was anyone left in the area, and they knew they were in trouble, they might make for the old Spanish fort at the one, or the mission at the other. Both had walls and water, and when the chips were down, that was what mattered.

Night was falling fast, and he turned the big dun horse into a cove on the mountainside, where there was a sparse covering of brown, tough grass, hobbled him and the cavalry mount and let them do their best to get something out of it.

Apache Country

There was a covering of piñon pines, up here, and the patient saguaro, stretching their limbs up to the sky.

Then he made himself coffee on a capful of fire carefully shielded with flat stones.

The horses he picketed where he could see them, carefully checked the area around his campsite for snakes, and rolled up in his blankets, adding the saddle blanket to his bedroll. He rested his head on his saddle and roofed his head with his hat. Already, the stars were out, and the temperature on the high desert hillside was dropping fast.

FOUR

The sun was coming up over the mountains and Rosemary was making breakfast. Darker and his men were already saddling up their horses, and Japhet and Babs were bringing in the horses for the wagons.

Rory and his sister laid out the plates on the two boxes that served them as a table, and Rosemary devoted herself to tending the big coffee pot and the two frying pans she needed to make the bacon and beans. She had made biscuits the night before and they were in a basket on the tail of the wagon which carried the food supplies. Cisco leaned over her shoulder and helped himself to a biscuit, and looked approvingly at the neatly stocked larder built into the back of the wagon.

'Sugar, flour, bacon, coffee,' he counted off. 'Well-stocked kitchen you're running here, little lady! I like a woman knows her way around.'

Rosemary picked up the big kitchen knife she used for slicing the bacon, and pulled the half flitch over towards her.

He noticed the manoeuvre, and grinned.

Apache Country

'Time could come, you'll be happy to stay close to Cisco,' he said. 'I smell a whole lot better'n an Apache, any day!'

'Better, maybe,' she said, 'but not a whole lot. Now get out of my way!'

His face darkened, and for the first time she saw the ugliness come through.

'You better learn better manners, li'l lady, and fast!' he said.

But he stepped back to one side, and let her walk to the fire where the pans were sizzling.

She pushed the long iron bar she used as a poker and kitchen tool into the fire to one side, and started to fry the bacon. Her jar of beans was ready on the table to go into the bacon fat, and she checked that the big, steel spoon was within reach. If it came to a fight, she meant to leave her mark on any of the men who came near her.

Overnight, the atmosphere had changed. Last night, there was a feeling of tension and expectation about the three men, which even the good-hearted Japhet had noticed. She saw him glance across the fire at Babs, and saw with some relief that Babs had a tell-tale bulge in the bunched folds of her skirt. She hoped Babs had taken her warning to heart, that the bulge was a gun, and that the gun was loaded.

This morning, there was a definite feeling of menace about them. They were jumpy, as though they knew something was about to happen, but did not know exactly when. Even the thin veneer of civilization on Brennan was gone. The man was peremptory and surly.

Apache Country

The children were her main worry. The three adults did not stand much of a chance if the three riders turned nasty, but there was at least some chance since they were all armed. She saw this morning that Japhet's Winchester had been shifted to the side of the wagon where he leaned, sipping coffee from a tin mug, and that it was only inches from his hand. The shotgun, which normally rode beside the wagon seat, was no longer visible. She hoped Japhet had moved it and not one of the men.

But the children made them vulnerable. If they were threatened, the adults would have to do whatever the men wanted. And she was positive Darker, in particular, would not hesitate to use that vulnerability.

There were trees and cactus all around them and when she raised her eyes to the ramparts of the mountains, she could see a deep carved notch which she assumed to be a pass. Along the flank of the range, she could see a fuzzy, yellowish blob, some miles away, which she suspected were cottonwoods. Where there were cottonwoods, there was usually water, so she wondered why they had not pushed on last night to camp there.

She poured the beans into the pan, and stirred them around with a spoon to heat them up, then stood up and called out, 'Come and get it!'

She had always been able to raise the echoes when she felt like it, and it felt good to let off some of the tension by raising them now. Her voice bounced off the cliffs, and the horses tossed their heads and stamped, unsettled. She was used to

Apache Country

people being surprised at the sheer volume, but even she was amazed at the effect on the three gunmen.

Darker spun round as though she had hit him with a hot iron, and the other two jerked spasmodically.

'Fer Christ's sake, woman!' Darker snarled. 'Keep yer goddamn voice down!'

Cisco was scowling, and Brennan swore under his breath. Both of them were looking anxiously out to the south, where the mountains faded into the desert.

She stared at him. 'What's the trouble?'

'Trouble? Apaches the goddamn trouble. Apaches and Pimas and Papagos and every damn kind of Injun between here and the Mexican border's the trouble! Keep the noise down. Cisco?'

'No dust, but we better hurry.'

'Eat yer vittles, and get into the saddle. And you, Davey! Harness up and let's get these wagons on the road. We got twenty miles to do today.'

He had been peremptory before, but had never stepped over the bounds to give a direct order. Japhet and Babs were as astounded as Rosemary herself. Japhet stood up and started forward.

'Now, see here, Darker, We were happy enough to have your company to Nogales, but—'

Darker turned on him.

'Shut yer mouth,' he snarled. 'These wagons ain't goin' nowhere near Mexico. They're goin' where I'm goin', and, if you know what's good for you, so are you!'

Japhet reached out for the Winchester, and

Apache Country

Darker struck him hard in the face, knocking him sprawling. Cisco and Brennan had guns in their hands, pointing them at the children and Babs. Rosemary, to one side, was ignored.

She wrapped a cloth round her hand, and reached out slowly to take hold of the end of the poker. By now, she could see, the end in the fire was red hot.

'Touch that rifle, and I'll kill you,' Darker told Japhet. The farmer, shocked, looked back at him through slitted eyes.

'What's this all about?' he asked. Rosemary was glad to notice that although he looked shaken, his voice was low and did not tremble.

'You'll see, soon enough. And if you and the little ladies behaves yourselves, maybe you'll live through it,' Cisco told him. 'Meantime, if you wanna stay parents, you better collect up the guns. Where's that shotgun as used to be up there by the wagon box?'

Japhet started to get to his feet, and stopped as Darker pulled his gun.

'Just so's we understand each other, mister, the kids die first,' he said. 'Just the guns, butt first, and down here in front of the wagons.'

Japhet might have chanced his luck with the rifle if it had been just him, and even just him and his wife, but the children were too much of a risk. He gathered the rifle and shotgun and brought them to where Darker indicated.

'You want me to smash 'em?' Brennan indicated the guns.

'Smash em? Hell, no. Apaches'll give good gold for them guns,' said Darker. 'And now the handguns.

Apache Country

Slow and careful, and maybe the kids'll see another sunrise.'

Japhet unfastened his coat and unbuckled his gunbelt, and dropped it into the pile.

'Now you!' Cisco was pointing at Babs. 'You got a bulge under that skirt wasn't there last night. Let's see what it is, now, quick!'

Equally helpless in the face of the threat to her children, Babs turned away to lift her skirt.

'None o' that! I wanna see what you're doing! Turn this way!' Brennan was enjoying himself, though in truth there was nothing to see except Babs's voluminous petticoats when she turned back. Like Rosemary, she was wearing a gunbelt with a Colt in it. She dropped the gun and then her skirt.

'And now you. . . .'

Cisco turned towards where Rosemary had been and stopped in his tracks. She had vanished, and the pan lay in the fire, fat spitting into the embers.

'Where'd she go?' Darker was thunderstruck. 'Brennan, you see her go?'

'Naw, I was watching momma here.' The big man looked frustrated and annoyed. 'Tell us where she went, blondie, right now!'

Babs had quite clearly no idea. She looked as shocked and surprised as the rest of them, and spread her hands helplessly.

'I never saw her move. I was too busy giving you the thrill of a lifetime,' she said bitterly.

Japhet just shook his head.

'How would I know?' he said. 'We hardly know the woman. Picked her up a couple of days out of

35

Apache Country

Tucson. She worked in a saloon up by Dead Man's Creek. Mining town. Wanted to come West, so I said she could work her way with us.'

The children stared at him with their mouths open. They had known Rosemary all their lives, and looked upon her as a favourite aunt. Japhet's scowl stopped the protests on their lips, and the three gunmen, staring into the desert for signs of the missing woman, missed the by-play.

'Come back here, you big cow!' Brennan bawled into the desert morning. 'Come back here, or I'll kill these kids, one by one!'

Babs cried out and ran to the children. Japhet looked as though he was going to throw himself at Brennan.

From the desert there came no reply.

Brennan raised his pistol, and Darker gestured at him, irritably.

'She ain't gonna come in for a pair of kids she only met a week ago,' he said. 'And we don't wanna make any more noise. We'll have Manolito on our necks quick enough as it is.'

Cisco climbed onto his horse, and stood in the stirrups, to look around. But he slumped back into the saddle shaking his head.

'Bitch!' he said, viciously. 'We'll have to catch her, though, Dark. She gets away and someone finds her, we'll swing. She can tell them who we are.'

'Someone finds us with the rifles, we'll swing whether she gets away or not,' Darker said. 'So the quicker we get this business over with, the better. We'll go and collect them now. Then on to the rendezvous.'

'All the same, I'd feel happier if we knew she was dead,' said Cisco.

Darker looked undecided. Then he nodded his head.

'You're the best tracker, and she can't have got far. Find her and kill her,' he said.

Babs sucked in a horrified breath and looked desperately at her husband.

'There's no need for that,' he protested, and Darker turned upon him a face to quell any argument.

Cisco helped get the horses harnessed up, and watched the little wagon-train start along the base of the mountains, then walked over to the fire. He could see Rosemary's boot prints clearly enough where she had stood by the wagons, and the trail leading from the wagon to the fire.

He rescued the pan from the embers, and dug some burned bacon out of it with his fingers, wincing at the heat, then threw the pan back into the ashes. True to his desert instincts, he drank from the coffee pot and poured the remaining coffee over the embers, which hissed and spat at him. All the same, he made sure they had been quenched.

All the time, his eyes were raking the desert, reading signs. He could see where Rosemary had stepped backward from the fire to the nearest stand of junipers, and then her trail to a big desert sumac where she had knelt, watching the camp. Then he followed her trail into the desert. She was making for the nearest flanks of the mountains, in direct

Apache Country

line with the notch which he knew contained the trail which led over into Blood Creek Basin. There was a sand spring in back there, and she would have water if she could find it.

He climbed onto the horse again and leaning low over the trail, he began the surprisingly difficult business of tracking down his prey. She was making good time – in fact, she could not have stopped moving since she had disappeared and confirmed to her own satisfaction that she was not immediately being followed.

For a while he was baffled that her footprints were so hard to find and strangely brushed over and blurred, until he realized she was trailing a petticoat behind her to obscure the trail. The discovery did not help him, much.

Several hours later, his speed restricted by the need to dismount and walk most of the time, he had still not come upon her. He was hot and angry, and he swore to himself he would make her pay for his hard work when he caught her.

He did not, of course, know that she had a gun.

Still less did he know he was being watched.

On the shoulder of the mountain above him, Murphy sat on his horse against a boulder and watched the desert below through field-glasses. He was careful to cup his gloved hands round the lenses of the glasses to avoid any chance of a reflection, even though he was in the shadow of the mountain.

He had missed the scene around the wagons, though he had seen the woman start her run into

Apache Country

the desert, and the subsequent panic and the departure of the wagons. Until he had seen the woman run away, he had been about to ride down onto the flat to warn the wagon master about the presence of Indians further down the trail he was following. But all was plainly not well. He watched Cisco climb onto his horse, and noted with some amusement the number of times he had to climb down again. The woman was making surprisingly good time, and keeping in a straight line which would bring her to the pass.

What she did not know was that the pass was steep, and exposed, and once she got to it, she would be visible to the horseman coming up behind her. Cisco was making a slow trail, but he was also on a horse and when he was mounted, he made much better time than she did.

Slowly but surely, he was catching up with her, and soon, within the next hour at least, she would emerge from the scrub and cactus of the desert onto the bare rocks of the pass. By that time, Cisco would be within range.

He considered for a moment the idea that the horseman might be aiming to rescue the woman, who might have run off for no good reason, but dismissed it because of her frantic attempts to conceal her trail.

In this wild and desolate place, anything might happen.

He was heading for Tubac and Tumacacori anyway, and he had to turn south after the wagons, so he would be following them.

Apache Country

If they were simply ill-advised homesteaders taking a chance on the Indians – a suicidal chance in the present state of the territory – he would be able to advise them and lead them to the army patrols which by this time should be coming south from Tucson.

On the other hand, loaded wagons making for the same place the Apache were heading could have other motives for making their journey. One way or another, he needed to keep an eye on them, and the woman would, at least, be able to give him information.

He swung the dun away from the rim, and began the slow descent over naked rock into the pass. The dun picked its way delicately, accustomed to moving on this surface, and the Army mount took confidence from it. He could hear it slip from time to time, but it followed the lead rein without balking.

And so, picking his way carefully and listening intently for the sound of other riders he came to the top of the pass and started down it.

FIVE

Rosemary was at the end of her tether when she got to the foot of the pass.

For the past hour, she had caught the occasional glimpse of her hunter, and she knew he was catching up despite everything she could do to slow him.

The heat was frightful. Cumbered with her heavy cotton petticoats, she was suffocating. She had torn one off and made herself a head covering earlier on, and it was effective enough. She had seen illustrations in magazines of the desert Arabs and the way they dressed, and was careful to keep her skin covered not only against sunburn, but also to cut down the amount of sweat she might lose.

She was used to not being wet with sweat. In this kind of heat the water evaporated as soon as it came through the skin, and it was natural to cover up as much as possible. But she was losing water all the same, and she had had nothing since morning except the coffee she had drunk while making breakfast.

She had snatched biscuits from the basket as she faded back into the desert, but her escape had been a matter of a split second while the gunmen's attention was distracted and the water skin might have sloshed as she moved it.

Now, all that was ahead of her was the bare rock of the pass. Had she time to climb to the first bend in the trail before the horseman behind her came into rifle range? She doubted it, but to stay here in the cactus would be the equivalent of giving up. He would find her, one way or the other.

Despite her care, she had picked up several thorns, though so far she had managed to avoid the dreaded cholla, the one the men called 'jumpin' cactus' because it was reputed to jump ten feet to stick its millions of thorns into the unguarded rump.

She decided to stake her life on the range at which she would be exposed. A man who had spent most of the morning climbing on and off a horse in this heat might well miss at long range, even without the shimmering atmospheric disturbance of the heat on the desert, which made any distant object swim and wobble. Before he got close enough up to make a certain shot, she hoped to be far enough up the pass to hide.

She got out the Colt and checked the loads. Like many careful people, her father had always carried the pistol with an empty chamber under the hammer in case it went off accidentally, but an accidental shot was the least of her problems, now. She loaded the empty chamber, and fastened the gunbelt around her waist over her skirt.

Then she started out of the cactus and up the trail which led into the throat of the pass. Once out on the rock apron to the pass, she glanced back. Her

Apache Country

pursuer was leaning out of his saddle, reading her trail, about a mile or so back. But even as she watched, he looked up, and saw her. Immediately, he kicked his horse into a run and she could see the rifle in his hand.

There was a broken side-wall to the pass a little further up, and she hurried towards it. At some time in the past, a huge wedge of rock had broken off from higher up and fallen into the canyon. There was room behind it for her to be out of sight, but also be able to watch Cisco as he came up the trail. With any luck, she could get the first shot in. If she made it count, she hoped she would be able to catch the horse, and provide herself with transport and, she prayed, a full canteen.

She raised the Colt, and thumbed back the hammer. She had been careful to keep the weapon cleaned and oiled and she was not a bad shot, but the barrel on this gun was meant for use at close range, and she could not risk a long-distance shot in case it warned him.

If he knew she had a gun, he would be wary, and she needed him confident and careless. She would get but one chance, so that one must be a winner.

Cisco saw her run behind the rock, and thought Rosemary was making an attempt to conceal herself. He grinned as he urged the horse up the trail, and reined him in next to the rock. Considering that the Apache were bound to be within hearing distance of gunfire, he was very wary of shooting. He was prepared to kill her with his bare hands or his knife, if he could. But there was

Apache Country

something he wanted first; that splendid body at his mercy.

'You might as well come out, li'l lady,' he said mockingly. 'If I have to come in after you, I'll make it hard for you. You be right nice to me, and I might even let you live.'

Rosemary did not reply. He was still too far away for a definite kill, and by accident, Cisco had stopped in her blind spot, directly down hill. If she kept quiet she might provoke him into coming closer. Ideally, she wanted him in the gap between rock and wall, where he could not jump out of the way.

She held the gun in both hands and pointed it towards the gap.

She heard the horse moving around, and then the creak of leather as he dismounted. Her breath was coming in short gasps, and she made a huge effort to control it. This shot she must not miss.

The next words, though, came from above her head.

'A gun! I didn't know you got a gun, or I'd a bin a bit more careful out in the cactus! Best you drop it now, though, li'l lady, or I'll have to shoot you straight through the head.'

Gasping, she turned her head round to look up. Cisco was standing on the rock above her head, the Winchester held loosely in his hands, looking down at her. The very narrowness of her refuge prevented her from spinning round in the cleft to fire at him. He had fairly caught her, and now, she knew, he would be merciless.

That he would kill her, she did not doubt. She

Apache Country

could not see how the gunmen could possibly leave their victims alive once they had shown their hands. Alive, they were witnesses; dead, merely another group of pilgrims who didn't make it. If they were missed it would not be for a long time, and there were so many reasons why migrant families disappeared, from Indians to drought.

There was only one tiny thing in her favour: because of the Indians, about whom he seemed to know rather more than he should, Cisco would only shoot if he was forced to. She, on the other hand, had nothing to lose by making noise. She started to move out of the cleft and into the pass, with the idea that she might be able to swing the gun to cover him.

Cisco was ahead of her, though. He dropped from the rock and ran, cat-footed round into the pass so that the Winchester was pointing at her as she came out.

'Drop it, you bitch, or I'll drop you, and damn the Chiricahuas!'

'Or then again, I jest might drop you. Be a helluva sight more fun,' said a pleasant voice from behind him.

Cisco swore, but he was careful to turn only his head.

Murphy watched him, mild eyed under the brim of his hat. He had the Smith & Wesson in his right hand, and he looked as though he meant every word.

'Cisco. Reckoned it was you, when I seen you from the rimrock,' he said conversationally. 'Thought you was warned off from this part of the country, after that last time you was trading with Cochise?'

Apache Country

'Army ain't got the right nor the men to keep me out,' said Cisco sullenly.

'I'm army,' said Murphy, simply. 'And I'm the man warned you off, last time. What you up to this time, sides abusin' a female and fixin' to murder her?'

Cisco started to sweat. No matter how rough Western men might be, none of them had any time for a man who misused women. He had seen one man hanged for it, and there were tales of men being burned.

'She was fixin' to shoot me!' he protested.

'Shows she got to know you right well in a short time,' said Murphy. 'And there ain't nothin' much wrong with her judgement, neither. Drop the Winchester and unfasten your gunbelt, Cisco.'

'You'll not leave me without a gun, out here?'

'Cisco, if you think I'd turn my back on you knowin' you had a gun, you've been drinkin' cactus juice again! Now, drop 'em and don't rile me more'n you are already. I don't hold with men as bothers womenfolk. Makes me real aggravated.'

The gunman dropped the rifle with a clatter, and unfastened his belt. Murphy holstered his pistol, and swung down from the dun, and for just a second his back was turned to the gunman.

'Look out!' Rosemary saw Cisco's hand grab for a second gun hidden at the back of his belt under his leather vest. Murphy turned, smooth as a jaguar, and his hand whipped down to his boot. For just a split second she thought she saw a shaft of pure sunlight pass between the two men.

Then Cisco was on his knees, the gun sliding

away down the rock slope, and blood running from his mouth. Just under his chin, a thick wooden peg seemed to have sprouted from his throat.

She felt sick at the strangled retching sound which came from the gaping mouth, while his fingers clasped at the wood. Then his eyes turned upwards, and he fell sideways onto the rock. For a few seconds, he threshed feebly, then his leg kicked out, and then relaxed.

It was so fast and so final that she could hardly believe she had watched it happen.

'Is. . . is he dead?' she said, realizing even as she said it that this was probably the silliest question she had asked in her life. The man was obviously and horribly dead.

'Well, he ain't whistlin' "Dixie",' said Murphy. 'Not many people survive a knife in the throat. Known fact.'

He reached down and pulled the knife from the corpse's neck.

'Never did have any kind o' judgement, Cisco. Me, I'da left the gun where it was until my attention was distracted, and then gone for it. Might 'a managed to get one into me before I got the steel into him.

'Funny how what goes aroun', comes aroun', ain't it? Got this knife offen a dead Apache yesterday, and it comes in useful for killin' a comanchero this mornin'. Seems almost like it was meant, don't it?'

He wiped the knife on Cisco's shirt, and went through his pockets quickly, then wiped his fingers on the dead man's clothing as well. He was left with a few coins, two of them gold, a notebook with a stub

Apache Country

of pencil tucked into it, a sack of tobacco and cigarette papers, and a metal box of matches.

'Not much to show for a life o' crime and violence, is it?' he said. 'Knew this man for best part of ten years, and never knew him with more than a price of a drink and a smoke in his poke, nor an honest idea in him.

'He's robbed and murdered all over the territory. he's traded whiskey with the Injuns, rustled cattle, held up the Butterfield Stage when it was runnin'. Never come up with the money to bless hisself with.'

She realized he was talking to let her regain her composure, and appreciated it.

'Trouble is, what we goin' to do with him?'

He looked around, speculating.

'He'll have to go into that cleft you used, ma'am. We can throw a few rocks on him, keep the buzzards off.'

'Buzzards?'

He pointed straight up, and she followed the direction until she could see a tiny speck moving in circles high above them in the blue.

'Old turkey buzzard up there, he c'n see right down here right now. When he's sure there's a meal in it for him, he's certain sure to come down here to eat. Another one over there' – he pointed – 'he'll see our buzzard here, and he'll come down to see what he's doin'. And the next, and the next and the next.'

She looked at Cisco's dead face and shuddered.

'Don't take on, ma'am,' said Murphy. 'Him bein' dead makes the world a cleaner place. Stand on me for that. Shoulda shot him years ago, but we wintered once together up in the Superstitions, and he was right good comp'ny just for those snow months. Not like the same man.'

'You knew him?'

'Big territory, ma'am, with very few people in it. White people, that is. Plenty Injuns, o' course. So the men who travel around get to know one another sooner or later. Bad and good. Men carry the news from one place to another.

'In a way, we live in a village, only real spread out. We all know each other, or we know of each other, and the news moves around, because, heck, there ain't much else to talk about when you're at a campfire or meet in a saloon.'

All the time he was talking he was wrapping the body in the blanket from the horse ridden by the Apache he had killed, and dragging it into the shadow of the rock.

'Why do you want to hide it?'

'Apache comes by here and finds a body, he knows there's at least one survivor, so he may come a-lookin' to see where we gone. I don't want to attract a mite more attention than I need to because I'm looking for those wagons you run from, to turn 'em back.'

Rosemary watched as he pulled his field-glasses from the saddle bag, and leaned on the saddle to keep them focused on the desert.

'Who. . . who are you?' she said. Apart from the fear when she was running from Cisco, and the shock at the speed of the events, she was still thoroughly keyed up. Things were going far too fast for

Apache Country

her, and she needed to regain control.

'Name's Murphy, ma'am,' he said, without looking round. 'Out scouting for the army, and tryin' to round up the ranchers and the pilgrims afore Natche does, or Manolito.

'Didn't know about your party, though. What're you doin'out here?'

'We were heading West until Japhet heard of the silver mines down in Mexico. Then we were heading south. We're from Mississippi. Heading for California, originally.'

'Better idea than the Mexican silver mines, any day,' he approved. 'Right unpleasant, some of them mines. They're a trap, to. There's plenty o' men looking to make their fortune. You get in there and good claims are all took up. Sit down for a while, and you've et up all your grub, and you can't get back.

'So, you take on a job at one of the mines at half pay, and then you're really stuck. Can't leave without your pay, can't get the pay to get out. Slave labour, them mines, but then they always was.

'Any case, they'd not take on your friend Japhet. He's married, and the mines employ only single guys. That way they don't have to look after widows.'

He finished tucking away the body, hung the dead man's gunbelt over the pommel of his saddle, and dropped his Bowie knife into a saddle-bag. He threw the Winchester to Rosemary.

'C'n you fire one o' these things, ma'am?'

Rosemary had been firing rifles all her life, and said so, sharply.

'Right, you look out for my back, and I'll look out

Apache Country

for yours. Now, mount up and we'll catch up with them wagons.'

He caught up the reins of the dead man's horse. It was a far better mount than the stolen cavalry horse, and he was glad to see Rosemary head straight for it. Showed she knew her horseflesh as well as her shooting.

'Now, do you reckon those friends of yours want to be catched up with, or not?'

She settled into Cisco's saddle, and gathered up the reins he handed to her.

'My friends certainly want it. But the men with them certainly won't. They joined up with us just outside Tucson, just sort of rode up and settled in. We never saw them before.'

She explained how the attitude of the unwanted riders had changed over the course of a few days. How they had guided the party away from the water of the Santa Cruz and the mission of San Xavier. How they seemed to be making for a rendezvous. Murphy sat silent while she talked, his eyes watching her carefully.

He had not yet decided whether she was trouble or not, but anybody pursued by Cisco got his vote, and he had heard the threats the man had been making, and believed them.

'Did you get their names?' he asked.

'Cisco you know. Brennan was another, and Darker. He was the leader, I think.'

He shook his head.

'Not heard of either of them. What d' they look like, ma'am?'

51

She described Darker's broad shoulders and heavy dark looks, and Brennan's thickset power and strength. Murphy's face cleared immediately.

'Ned Fuller and Jesse Carver,' he said. 'Bad actors, both. Heard they was running with the comancheros, though.'

Rosemary's horse slipped, and she automatically steadied him. Murphy noticed the instinctive reaction with approval. He had been dreading having to handle a hysterical female, but apart from looking a little dazed, she had dropped right into step.

'I heard people around Tucson talking about comancheros,' Rosemary said. 'I thought they must be some kind of Indian. But Cisco was not an Indian, was he?'

Murphy shook his head.

'Mexican father, German ma was what I heard,' he said. 'Quiet now. I'll tell you about comancheros later.'

He was listening intently, she saw. She tilted her head and tried to hear what he was hearing, but caught only the incessant whisper of the wind caressing the desert.

In fact, Murphy was listening for something rather than to it. The two of them with the led horse were down off the pass now, and skirting the foot of the mountains, among the desert plants. He noticed barrels and organ pipe cactus among the mesquite, the ubiquitous saguaros which marked out the Sonoran like sentinels, and broadleaf yucca so precious to the Apache who ate the fruit, made cords from the fibrous leaves and soap from the roots.

'Foller me,' he said quietly, and turned their horses' heads towards the mountains again. She followed, unquestioning.

Ahead, he knew, were the Apaches he had seen last night riding through the pass between the Santa Ritas and the Sycamores. Ahead, also, the hijacked wagons with Carver/Darker and Fuller/Brennan.

Coincidence? Or a rendezvous? He had to know before he ran for Tucson, and the patrol point, and that meant trailing or otherwise locating the wagons. Preferably before the Apache did.

SIX

Rosemary watched Murphy as he surveyed the desert once again through his field-glasses. She did not know what to make of this strange man who had ridden into her life in time to save it, yet killed without apparently feeling remorse, even for a man he admitted having known and, for a time at any rate, liked.

She was not stupid enough to feel any regret for the dead Cisco. Realistically, had Murphy not appeared, seemingly out of the very rocks, she would by now be abused and dead. She told herself she would have sold her life dearly, but she knew in the end Cisco would have had his way.

She sneaked another look at Murphy as he rose in his stirrups to put the field-glasses to his eyes again, and sweep the desert. Then, to her surprise, he pulled his boots out of the stirrups and stood upright on his saddle. The horse, whickering gently, braced itself against the shifting burden.

He was a solid man in his late thirties, wide-shouldered and narrow-hipped. Tall, he looked well over six feet. She was considered towering at five feet and ten inches, but she had to look up at him, even when he was not standing close to her.

Under his flat black hat, his eyes were a startling blue in the deeply tanned face. He wore a black wool shirt, dark jeans and a black leather vest fastened with a strap at the front. Round his neck was a dark-blue silk bandanna, very faded. His boots were well-worn and cactus-scarred but they had been good, finely stitched and of excellent quality.

His gunbelt was black and polished, and his trouser belt had a handsome silver buckle of the work she was beginning to recognize as Navajo. He had a silver bracelet on his left wrist of the same origin.

He dropped back into the saddle and put the field-glasses away.

'Tell me all about the things Brennan and Darker said. They must know they're takin' a hell of a chance movin' down that way.

She thought carefully before answering, then told him everything she knew.

'It wasn't so much what they said and did. There was always good reason for doing everything they did, and they always went out of their way to spell it out. It was their manner, their attitude.

'The further away from Tucson we got, the less they bothered to hide their contempt. It didn't seem reasonable. I mean, we've been on the trail a long time, now. We fought Indians. We had to deal with storms and we came across the Llano Estacado. We'd never have got this far if any of us had been

Apache Country

weak or cowardly. And they were treating us as if we were pathetic.'

'How'd they get the drop on you?' The question was mild, but his eyes were sharp under the hat.

'The children. Rory and Amanda. The gunmen threatened them. It was worse than having our hands tied.'

'Young 'uns? You got children on them wagons?'

'Sure. Babs and Japhet's children. They're just darling.'

'And dangerous. With them fer hostages, them friends o' yours got to do what they bin told. Dangerous.'

He gathered up the reins and they moved on.

'Another thing,' she said. 'They know there are Apache here. The further south we got, the more careful they was . . . were. When I shouted them to breakfast this morning, they all nearly had heart attacks.'

He chuckled.

'That was you? Thought the pass was gonna collapse. They's probably men riding from Phoenix this moment, wonderin' where that breakfast is, they was shouted to. Where'd you learn to shout like that?'

She coloured. 'I like to let it rip now and again,' she protested. 'Kind of lets out the pressure.'

'Purely does,' he grinned. 'I was thinkin' of comin' to join you my own self, when I seen you duck out and start to travellin'. You was makin' good time there for a while, too.'

'Until he caught up,' she said bitterly.

Apache Country

'You'd 'a' done better to circle back and wait for him. You could 'a got him from close up as he come past,' he said. 'Still, you done fine by me. Anythin' else happen?'

'Well, they seemed to be heading for a meeting with somebody,' she said doubtfully. 'They were in a hurry at one point and afraid they were not going to make it in time. Darker also said something about Apaches. He said they would pay a good price for Japhet's guns.'

One memory prompted another.

'As I was going off, I heard . . . Darker, I think it was. He said they would be hanged anyway if anyone found them with the rifles. I mean, they haven't got any rifles but their own. Nice rifles, though. They looked new.'

Murphy glanced sharply at the Winchester in the boot attached to Cisco's saddle. It was indeed a new Winchester, and he reached over and pulled it out to look at it more closely.

'I heard the cavalry was gonna get some of these, some time soon,' he said. 'This one's got a gov'mint mark on it. See here!'

He pointed at the mark stamped into the breech of the rifle. She leaned over and looked at it, and caught the smell of the man, sweat and woodsmoke, leather and horse all mingled. It smelled strong and basic, and stirred something within her.

Murphy passed her his canteen, then took a long slow drink himself, rinsing it around his mouth before swallowing it. Next stop, he must water the horses.

Apache Country

He knew that to the girl, he looked unconcerned, but, in fact, deep down, he was deeply worried. The wagons were plainly being driven, fairly fast, towards Tubac.

It made no sense for the comancheros to be making for the tiny settlement unless they knew it to be safe at least so far as they were concerned. That meant that there would not be people there. Or that there were so few they did not have to worry.

That, in turn, meant that something had happened there. The old Presidio, built by the Spanish, had been burned down and rebuilt several times already, and the garrison had been moved out long ago. But when last he heard, the fort itself was still intact, and there was a saloon and a couple of families settled there in stout, adobe houses.

He was counting on the waterhole there for his horses and himself, and if the gunmen were sitting on it, then the waterhole would be hard to reach.

He was also worried about the fate of the wagon party. Certainly the comancheros would not allow them to escape to bear witness, so at the moment they appeared to be valuable, at least for driving the wagons.

But he could not work out what Darker – Carver – wanted the wagons for. That he might want the women, Murphy could understand. Women were always valuable in the comanchero world. The man and the children would be nothing but an encumbrance except as a way of bending the woman to his will.

Maybe the outlaw joined the party in order to get

the wagons, as he could as easily have mounted the party on their draught-animals and made much better time. Carver wanted the wagons, perhaps because of what they contained.

He turned south again, towards the border, Tubac and the unknown fate of the wagons and the Davey party. He had a growing uneasy feeling of events moving too fast for him.

Also, the wind was rising, and high winds on this stretch of desert meant a dust storm. A storm would delay him because he would have to hole up and wait it out, while the dust would wipe out the tracks he was following. And that, in turn, meant he would have to count on the wagons calling at Tubac.

SEVEN

Murphy thought he detected a change in the wind sound, and allowed himself a peek out of the blanket tent he had erected between the two huge boulders. Their horses were standing where he had left them, shrouded and hobbled, and tucked up against the boulder. There was definitely a slight clearing of the air, and he could make out the shapes of the saguaro nearest the rocks, now.

The storm had, as usual, appeared to come out of nowhere and filled the air with dust. His only consolation was that it must have held up the wagons just as badly as it had held up him.

Rosemary coughed behind him, and his own reflex made him cough in sympathy. He leaned outside the tent, coughed and spat the dust out of his lungs into the settling sand. His mouth was so dry that no spittle came, and he took the stopper out of his water skin and poured some into a tin cup for the woman, then swilled out his own mouth and spat the water into the dust. It evaporated almost as he watched.

Apache Country

Rosemary uncurled from the bundle of blanket she had made of herself. Her dark hair was tousled, her cheeks red and her eyes sparkling.

'That was some storm!' she said.

'You look like you enjoyed it,' he said, amazed.

'I like storms, so long as I have shelter,' she said warmly. 'They make me feel more alive.'

The word jolted a memory, and her eyes darkened.

'I hope Japhet and Babs made it,' she said soberly. 'The kids will have been terrified.'

'Let's go see,' he said. Cautiously, he counted the saguaro and the clumps of vegetation he had checked before the storm had set in with its full savagery.

'What are you doing?' she said.

'Checkin',' he said briefly. 'See if we grew an extra rock or cactus in the storm.'

'Grew another. . .?'

'Yeah,' he said. He had come to the conclusion that nothing had been added to the landscape within his field of vision while his back was turned. 'You find an extra one, you shoot it. Friendly rocks don't creep around in dust storms.'

He put the saddle on the big horse which had been Cisco's and made a stirrup for her to mount.

'How will you find the wagons?' she asked, from the saddle. 'The sandstorm must have blown out the trail, surely?'

'They's up wind of us,'he said.

'How can you know that?' she asked.

'Don't get many cushions blowin' around in the

Apache Country

Sonoran all on their lonesome,' he said, drily.

He reached into an organ-pipe cactus clump and tore out a blue and white chequered cushion, its stuffing sadly spewing from the torn cover.

'That's one of Babs's covers,' said Rosemary, before she could stop herself.

'Figured so,' he said, throwing it to her. 'T'aint Apache. T'aint Pima, t'aint Papago. So I reckoned it had to be Davey. Blew here durin' the storm. Line up this with the wind direction, and we know—'

'Where they must be!' she said excitedly.

He shook his head. 'Where they was when the storm struck. Storm's over. If they ain't dead, they'll have moved along, now.'

'Which way?' she asked.

He shook his reins and started to lead the way.

'That's fer them to know and us to find out, ma'am,' he said. He was rolling a cigarette as he rode, and she followed him along obediently. She noticed his line of march was angling towards the ramparts of the mountains to the east. She considered for a moment, then decided he actually had a pretty shrewd idea where the wagons were headed.

When he was ready to tell her, she supposed he would. She was surprised to find she was happily confident about that.

EIGHT

Murphy rode loose in the saddle. Darker had been making good time when the storm struck, and Murphy reckoned the outlaw would have kept his wagons moving as long as he could before stopping. Even so, it made sense to assume they had overhauled him considerably, and act accordingly.

He drew the Winchester from the saddle boot, checked its action and made sure no dust had got into the chamber. It was fully loaded. He rode with it across his knees. He wondered about the Apache, too; what they had in mind and, above all, where they were. He kept on coming back to the rifles.

Murphy thought of those new army rifles and didn't want to speculate where they had come from. He had no knowledge of a shipment coming anywhere near, but then, who would bother to tell an army scout?

They picked up the trail of the wagons in the middle of the morning, and he read the story it had to tell: the overnight camp amid the ruins of the family's possessions; the looted chests, with clothes

Apache Country

spilling out into the sand; the cast-iron stove; the beds and drawers, broken and lying awry among the cactus. The outlaws had taken advantage of the storm to lighten the wagons.

Rosemary made a bundle of what she could salvage, and climbed back onto her horse. Murphy watched her without comment, and moved out as soon as she had remounted.

A few miles along, moving cautiously, he also found the story of a disaster. One of the wagons had run over a rock, and fallen on its side. In doing so, it had broken a water butt. The staves and bent hoops were lying in the sand.

'How much water was you carryin'?'

Rosemary knew what a broken butt meant as well as he did.

'Not enough for three extra mouths and horses,' she said. 'Not even enough for two. Another butt, and whatever they had on the wagons in skins.'

Murphy chewed on a match.

'And they'll not have picked up none last night in the storm. They ain't even bin nowhere near a water hole,' he said. 'No more have we, o' course. We need it by the time we get to Tubac, or the horses'll suffer. I've a notion to visit a tank I know, as well. Mebbe we'll find comp'ny there.'

He swung the horses to the south, and picked up the pace to a fast canter through the desert scrub. In the heat, the horizon wavered, making the mountains quiver like an uneasy sea.

Rosemary pulled her hat down over her forehead and squinted against the glare.

Apache Country

'Can it get any hotter?' she asked.

Murphy grinned. 'You shoulda bin here las' summer,' he said. 'We had a light thaw come June, and a feller I met in Phoenix told me you could fry an egg on the sidewalk in Yuma.'

He pulled up to perform his curious leap to stand on his own saddle and sweep the horizon with his binoculars.

'Trick the gauchos use in South America,' he said, when he caught Rosemary watching him with her wonder on her face. 'Gives you an extra mile, they calculate.'

'You've travelled,' she said.

'Travellin' kind of a man,' he agreed, dryly. 'It's in my nature, I reckon.'

They trotted on at an easy pace which also ate up the miles, until he turned away from the wagon tracks, and led her down into a gully between immense boulders. To her surprise, at the bottom of the boulders, in the shade, there was a small, clear pool of water.

He motioned to her to drink, and she threw herself full length and drank her fill, plunging her face into the surprisingly cool water.

When she had finished, he filled the water skins and their canteens before he himself drank, and then led the horses to the pool. The water was no lower when they had finished than when they started, though the pool itself was no more than four yards across.

'It's a tank, and the water is all in the sand,' he explained.

Apache Country

'How did you know it was there?'

'I was running powerful low one time, an' I saw a bee goin' into the rocks. Then I seen another. Bees need water even more'n we do. I calculated there might be a supply here, an' there was. Drops a mite lower in the hot times, gets a mite higher in the rainy season, but she's always there.'

'The rainy season?' She looked around at the unrelenting rock and cactus of the desert.

'Sure, July and August, all hell breaks loose out here. Depends on the heat, though. I seen storm clouds pourin' rain down here, and it was so hot, the water never got to the ground.'

'Do the Indians know of this place?'

'You can bet on that. Bin a place for people here since before the Spanish, I calculate. They's some rock carvin's back up there a piece, and some o' them cliff houses, up towards Casa Grande. Come from a long time back. The Indians won't go in them. Call 'em ghost houses. I hid in them one time.'

He swung into the saddle again, and led the way out into the desert.

Japhet hauled on the reins and cursed in a low bitter tone. The team threw itself into the harness, and the wagon creaked and bounced over the ground.

They had called at Tubac and it had been his best chance yet to free them from the outlaws, but he had been tied as thoroughly as a steer. All his great strength had been to no avail. Bound and gagged, he had been thrown under blankets in the back of his

Apache Country

own wagon while Brennan drove them into the almost deserted settlement.

Even if he had managed to break free, he knew in his mind his hands would have been as securely tied because Darker was riding with Babs and the children. And, by now, he was perfectly convinced that Darker would kill without a thought if he were threatened.

So Brennan drove the wagon and, when they rattled into Tubac, introduced himself as Babs's husband, while Japhet lay silent.

The men had been wildly angry when the wagon had fallen over and broken the water butt.

By chance, it happened to be the full butt on which they had been relying. Wherever they were planning to go, they needed water to get there, and after a hurried conference, they had decided on Tubac.

'Army's taken the sojers to Tucson anyway,' Brennan pointed out. Darker shot him an irritated look.

'But they got patrols out to bring the ranchers in,' he said. 'Could be a patrol in the old fort. Be the place they'd feel safe.'

But in the end they had no choice, so with Japhet bound and gagged and his wife terrorized into holding her tongue, to Tubac they had gone.

Japhet had no idea what happened there, but he had heard the voices, and the surviving water butt had been refilled, because he heard them slopping water into it. There had been laughter and some bad language, too, but he had no idea what it was about.

Apache Country

Half an hour after they had left Tubac, his blankets had been pulled aside, and Brennan let him out and motioned him back to the driver's seat. He was not allowed to speak to Babs, though she gave him an encouraging smile when he looked back her way, and then the outlaws were urging them onwards again.

From the sun, he knew they had swung wide and were heading for the mountains once again. But the diversion had taken a lot of time, and Darker's temper was worse than ever.

And now, night was coming on.

There was, however, an important new development in the situation, of which the outlaws knew nothing.

During the scrambling about to change drivers, Japhet had acquired a knife.

NINE

As he saddled up to leave Tubac, Murphy had to admit to himself that he was flummoxed by the woman he had picked up. She had been unmoved when they found the little settlement largely abandoned apart from Fat Cas Pearce and his Mexican-Apache woman in the ramshackle saloon they had made out of the old stage station. Pearce was amiable enough, though he prided himself on never passing on information about his customers, but Rosemary had wheedled all the information they needed out of Conchita.

Yes, the wagons had been here. Yes, there was a blonde woman and two children, but she had not seen Japhet anywhere. Brennan was driving one wagon, Babs the other. They had watered and moved on.

He was beginning to wonder who needed rescuing most. Like most western men, he knew that the idea of woman as a shrinking flower was hogwash. But he was seeing a side to womanhood he had never seen before. Rosemary's determination to catch up with the wagons and rescue what she called her family was as great as his own.

He tightened the cinches as Rosemary swung into the saddle, he caught the rifle she tossed to him, and climbed onto his own horse. The rest, a feed and the water from the trough outside had given the mounts new life.

He led off across the wash, reading the trail in the loose sand as easily as he would in daylight. The moon laid a sheet of white light across the desert and turned the duns and greens of the land and scrub into shades of silver and midnight.

As he had expected, they were able to follow the trail at a fast walk which was certainly quicker across the ground than the wagons. The ruts made by the wheels were plain to read – easier, even, because the light fell sideways across them and threw them into sharply defined shadow, like two black rails laid across the land.

The lay of the land, too, dictated where the wagons could go. The closer they got to the mountains, the more broken the land became, preparing to become first foothills and then canyons and rocks.

He speeded up, deliberately pushing the horses because in the night, he needed to worry less about the Apache. They were reluctant to travel at night. Not totally unwilling, but reluctant. On the other hand, if they had strong reason, they might, so every now and again, he pulled up to listen and look carefully around. He was careful to restrict his gaucho trick to occasions when he was up against some tall natural feature. The sleepiest sentry would be alerted if he saw a man suddenly appear out of the scrub and start staring around.

He was wrong to be confident.

Luckily, he heard the rattle of the ponies' hoofs during one of their silent breaks.

It came from away to their front, where the trail swung over some flat rocks and disappeared into a narrow gap between boulders. The rocks rose up, here, into a wall which crossed their path, and the blackness of the gap was the only obvious way through. The sounds told him two things – that the horses were unshod, which meant they were Indian ponies; and that there were several of them.

He dismounted and held the nostrils of his own horse, and gestured at Rosemary to do the same – pointlessly, he noticed wryly, because she had already leaned forward and clamped her hands over the horse's muzzle.

But neither of them had a hand for the cavalry mount and, out of the corner of his eye, Murphy saw it raise its head. He lunged for it, but got his hand on the bridle just too late to prevent it sending a whickering call into the night.

Instantly, the sound of the Indian ponies stopped. Out there in the desert, keen ears were being cocked. Senses already sharpened by the night and their own nerves were straining to catch the slightest hint of another clue to where the horse was calling from.

Stay where they were, and they were dead: run and they would betray themselves.

Or maybe not. If they weren't running, they would

be harder to find. He urged Rosemary out of the saddle, and pulled her horse down onto the ground, then showed her how to hold it down.

He shrugged out of his own jacket and wrapped it tightly round his horse's head, then pulled it, too, to the ground. Blinded, and with its hearing dulled, the horse lay silent, while Murphy grabbed the cavalry mount, pulled its saddle sideways, and slashed the cinch free.

Then he pointed it towards the rocks and, with a muttered apology, stuck the point of his knife into its rump.

The horse went off with an indignant whinny and ran crashing through the cactus, picking up speed all the time.

Murphy fell across his own horse, holding down its neck, and waited.

In seconds, there were yells from the rocks, and he could hear through the ground the sound of horses running. They were running further and further away, he hoped in pursuit of the running cavalry horse. When they caught it, they would find evidence of a successful ambush somewhere off in the night.

If they were on their way, as he feared, to a rendezvous with the wagons, they would return to the narrow canyon and their journey. Or, they might backtrack the horse to find its former rider. In that case, he and Rosemary had a choice: run or fight. He was aware that they were unlikely to survive either.

The trick worked, though, and the sounds of pursuit died away and finally stopped. He heard

Apache Country

confused hoofbeats through the ground, and a rattle of hoofs as the Apache crossed the rocks again. Then silence.

After a period, he let the horses up and he and the woman remounted and cautiously pushed on.

Now, the moonlight worked against them. Where it had picked out the wheel ruts in the desert, it turned the rock a uniform black and silver. Where scrape marks from the iron tyres would have showed up in sunlight, they simply vanished in the moonlight.

He gambled that the wagons would have to go through the slot ahead of them, and that the Apache had followed. At the other side of the slot, the ground rose steeply. The narrow pass was floored with sand washed down when the rains funnelled through this slender gap, and the horses' hoofs fell silent as they passed from the rock onto the fine powder.

Within the slot, the rocks were weathered into fantastic shapes, curving and bellying like sails set in the wind. The moonlight was striking vertically, making the place mainly black with a twisting silver ribbon along its floor. Imagination crowded the shadows with crouching Apaches, bows drawn and arrows pointing, but nothing moved except their muffled hoofbeats and the occasional whisper of cascading sand. Murphy wondered that he had never come across the narrow canyon before. He prided himself on knowing the local mountains passably well, and he had never even heard tell of it. If he had not been led to it by the fugitives, he would have remained ignorant. But he also knew that the mountains of Arizona were full of such hidden places. Without them, how could Cochise and Geronimo disappear into the Dragoons, and defy regiments to find them?

The canyon led upwards for nearly half a mile before the sight of a vertical bright slit ahead warned that they were about to emerge. He stopped the horses and slid to the ground. Warning Rosemary with a hand gesture to stay back, and keeping to the shadow, he inched his way to the mouth of the slot and risked a look out.

The moon was setting and the bottom of the valley in front of him was already in black shadow. Across the width of the valley from him, he could see the far rim back-lit, and he knew that he, and the mouth of the canyon, too, were bathed in it.

The valley was suspended in the hills, ringed by higher mountains, walled with cliffs like a vast footprint sunk into the rock. The trail wound away in front of him, for a while still climbing until it hit the valley floor.

From either side, cracks in the rocks ran down to this point. He waited for a few minutes until the shadow of the far wall began to climb up to him, dropping the cleft into darkness, and then walked forward to the brow of the rocks ahead. There was no need to try and track the wagons and the Apache now. There was no other way for them, except to follow the shelf of rock which swooped into the darkness.

On his level, as he looked cautiously from the

Apache Country

brow, were the tops of pines, and far away below him he could hear the soft sound of falling water. His horse, behind him in the slot, whickered gently as the smell of the water came to its nostrils, and he stepped back and stroked its nose absent-mindedly.

Rosemary touched him gently on the shoulder. He could smell her, a warm fragrance in the dark. A smell of the desert, spicy and sweet from the dust.

'What's out there?' she asked, softly.

'Hangin' valley,' he told her. 'On'y one way down, one way up, I reckon. They're all along the bottom, and I can't see that far. Moon's goin'.'

Down in the dark, Japhet sat with his back to the wagon wheel, his hands tied behind him. He was rubbing the rope methodically up and down the rough iron of the tyre, and he could feel it abrading between his wrists. Before morning, he would be free. Though what good it would do him was hard to say.

The journey here had been hard and exhausting, almost as much from the difficulty he had keeping his temper and his hands off Brennan as from the actual physical work. He had been driving these wagons for more than a thousand miles already, after all, and he was no stranger to hard work. He had been doing back-breaking labour since he had been able to walk. But the behaviour of the men who held him and his family captive puzzled and annoyed him. Darker was having difficulty keeping Brennan away from Babs, he could tell, although

Apache Country

why he bothered Japhet did not know. There were no witnesses and while they held the children, there would be little he could do.

He had obeyed all his instructions, but he had also managed to make preparations for escape as soon as the opportunity presented itself. There was a knife, now, in his boot and a second, smaller blade in the lining of his hat.

He had filled a canteen and hung it under the wagon tongue at their last stop, when the light was failing. There were hard baked biscuits tucked into the front of his shirt and in his pockets. Occasionally, he pretended to gnaw on one as he drove, to cover his actions in stealing them from his own store. Eating them was like gnawing on wood, but they would sustain the family, he knew, while they fled.

The darkness around him was complete. Darker and Brennan had been all business when they led him and the horses into the tunnel which led to this cave, and he had little time to do anything but unhitch the horses and quarter them in a side cavern before he had been tied and left, and the lanterns withdrawn.

Babs and the children had been taken away, but nothing else had been said. What his future held he did not know, save that it was unlikely that he was intended to survive it.

Before they had taken her away, he had time to say to Babs: 'No matter what happens, survive, and I will come for you. Remember, survive, and I will come for you.' Then all was darkness and his own

Apache Country

imagination. In the silence, things rustled and he could hear the horses, far away, moving and occasionally stamping.

He sat, and chafed at his bonds, and within him a mighty anger was rising.

Murphy led the horses down the trail, treading carefully and keeping an ear cocked for Rosemary, behind him.

She kept pace with him, yet she must by now be beyond exhaustion. He heard her stumble more than once before they reached the pines, and he led off to one side so that they would be off the trail when the sun came up.

The sky was in that peculiarly solid state of blackness which comes just before the dawning, and the desert stars were blazing like lanterns. If they were to rest, it had to be now because once the light came, he must move forward, and while he moved, he must avoid the Apache.

He found a small clearing, caused by the fall of a mighty tree, which had both brought down smaller neighbours, and created a small corral roofed with branches.

He pulled up, loosened the cinches on the horses, put a bait of corn into their nose-bags, and let them drink out of his hat. There was not much left in the water bags, but he could hear water somewhere in the valley, and he counted on being able to replenish his store soon.

Rosemary sat on the ground with her back to a tree and was instantly asleep. He covered her with a blanket, wound one round himself and sat between the trail and the corral, longing for coffee.

Slowly, the sky to the east lightened until it was a dove grey, and revealed puffy clouds, drifting to the west. While he watched, they turned first a light copper, and then a fiery red as the sun rose.

Once again, he was struck by the beauty of the land he lived in. The savage outlines of the mountains, the raw colour in the rocks, slowly coming to life with the birth of the new day, the smell of the pines and, above it all, the dusty, spicy breath of the desert even in this high valley.

There were tiny movements in the forest. The small creatures of the night were making their way home to hide from the daylight. Something small ran over his foot, feet pattering on the dusty leather, without breaking step. Wings flapped in the branches above him, and something swept low across the clearing and into the trees on the far side. He heard Rosemary wake, then stir. There was a silence as she looked around and then he heard quite distinctly the catch of breath when she could not see him.

He pursed his lips and whistled, low and sweet, and she made her way to him, and crouched.

'Hear anything?'

'Nothin' to hear. But they's down there, somewheres.'

He gestured with the Winchester towards the trail. Through the tops of the trees, he could see that the ground dropped away to the far side of the valley

Apache Country

towards the creek. Maybe that was where the Apache had been heading when he cut their trail. Maybe they had nothing to do with the wagons.

They caught up the horses, and he settled the saddles and led the way, riding down towards the water.

They rode down the slender track carrying their rifles in hand, Rosemary patiently jogging along behind. When he glanced at her from time to time, she was looking around, over his head, back along the way they had come, into the trees on either hand. No need to worry about the back trail with her there.

'Something bothering you?' she said.

'Yeah.' He dropped from the saddle, hunkered down on his heels, and tipped his hat over his eyes to have a good scratch. When Murphy got to thinking, a scratch seemed to help, as if he were rearranging the facts in his head.

'What's the matter?'

'Waal,' he said, scratching furiously, 'if them Injuns want to catch up with them wagons, they ain't tryin' mortal hard to succeed. Just moseyin' along here like a Sunday-school party, takin' their time and indulgin' in light conversation, I'd say.'

'Perhaps they don't know about the wagons? It must have been very dark by the time they got into this valley last night.'

'Possible.' But he did not think it was probable. The Apache had been travelling at night when it was not their habit. And if he could follow the wagons in the moonlight, he was darned sure the

Apache could. Murphy had served with an old buffalo hunter who swore an Apache tracker could track birds through the air and fish through the water, and he had never come across anything to make him disbelieve the old man.

No, these Apache were following the wagons, but did not want to catch them up. Just keep on their trail. So they expected to get something which the wagons were going after, and which was worth more to them than the chance to kill and rape. The Apache had no use for gold, and the contents of the wagons had already been tipped out in the desert.

Moving as carefully as he could, he led on after the group. It was a ticklish hunt, complicated by the fact that he had all the time to worry about Rosemary. Not worry, he corrected himself. The woman was more of an asset than a worry. What he had to do all the time was *remember* Rosemary and allow for two people rather than one.

On the other hand, he did not have to watch his back trail quite so carefully. He never allowed himself to rely totally on somebody else, but at the moment, he was coming as close as ever he had.

They followed the trail on down through the woods until he could see the gleam of water ahead and the sound of it filled their ears. The horses were straining eagerly towards it, and it took all his control not to let them have their heads.

He slipped from the horse and scouted ahead. In front of them, a waterfall dropped like a stream of liquid silver from the top of the cliffs into a bowl ringed with rocks, and floored with red sand. The

Apache Country

bowl's outlet ran away along the foot of their cliffs to the north, a gurgling, busy shallow stream running over a pebble bed.

At his side of the water, there was a wide strand of red sand fringed with tufts of grass, which stretched back into the wood. Further to the north, he could see that the trees fell back leaving a wide meadow, before crowding in again far away where the stream seemed to disappear below the cliffs.

They must be high above the desert here, and the air was actually a little fresher, though the sun still struck strongly down.

There was no sign of either wagons or Indians. No tracks in the sand, no horse droppings, no sign of the woodsmoke smell which would have meant a camp nearby. The groups they had been tracking seemed to have risen into the air and dissolved.

Careful to walk only on the rocks which occasionally appeared above the sand, he circled the basin, checking for tracks.

Not a thing.

He took off his hat and scratched to his heart's content, without producing a single thought. Three men, a woman and two children, two wagons and a war party of Apache had ridden into this hidden valley and, in a setting of heart-stopping beauty, had just vanished.

TEN

His hands were free, and he was armed with a knife. Now was the time, Japhet reckoned, to start controlling events himself.

He fumbled in his pockets and brought out his matches, wrapped in a twist of oilskin and tied with a thong. In the other pocket was a stub of candle, and he knew where there were others in the wagon.

He struck a light, and lit the candle. Then he sat back and held his hands over his eyes until the pain had gone away. Looking into a naked flame was like driving pins into his eyeballs, and the ache ebbed only slowly.

He stood and walked slowly and carefully about the wagon. He could see the entrance through which he and the wagon had been brought, away behind it. The cave where the horses were being kept was outside there, and the passage up which they had been driven kinked just beyond it, so no light from his candle would reach the outer cavern.

He equipped himself with a bundle of candles

from the box under the wagon seat, retrieved the canteen from the tongue, and filled his pockets with matches and more biscuit.

Then he started to retrace his steps towards the entrance.

When he came to a gallery, he marked the entrance with candle smoke, and passed on. The flame began to flicker, then to waver and finally a strong gust of wind blew it right out. He was fumbling with his matches to relight it when he heard, close by, the unmistakable sound of a man's snore. In the darkness, he also began to notice that the gloom seemed to be thinning, like a fog burning off with the sun. He waited, poised by a buttress of rock in the cavern wall, and very slowly, details began to come out of the blackness to him.

He could see the black outline of an archway ahead, beyond which was a much lighter area. He made his way cautiously round the buttress, looking carefully around him, and suddenly was able to see much more clearly.

Another snore.

To his left, a low archway was brightly lit and the sound of falling water came loudly through it. He crept along the wall towards the light and was almost there when he realized that what he had thought to be part of the cavern wall was, in fact, a pair of booted legs, belonging to a man who was standing just within the low arch. He was leaning forward to stare through the arch into the sunlight beyond.

Japhet stood still against the wall while he looked around him even more carefully. When the watcher

Apache Country

turned and looked behind him into the darkness of the cave, he would effectively be blind, so Japhet knew he had a small advantage.

He was halfway across the tunnel floor before it occurred to him that he had not actually seen this man before.

He was considerably more slender than Brennan and taller than Darker, and he wore clothes which were decorated with beads and feathers down the seams. His hat, which had a feather in the band, was hanging down his back on its thong, and his hair was almost white blond.

Japhet drew back into the crevices of the side of the cave while he considered the new situation. He had assumed that he had only to eliminate one of the outlaws, take his gun and shoot the other, then he could go looking for his family. It was a measure of how much the past couple of days had toughened him that he could consider the two killings so calmly.

Now, he had no idea how many men he faced. A shot might bring a dozen men running, and he could certainly not handle more than two at once. He grinned to himself at the thought. In a straight gunfight, he could not even handle one of them.

He was about to move again, when he heard a footstep from the inner cave behind him, and a man walked past in the shadow, making no effort to conceal himself. The newcomer had a Winchester over his arm, and was buckling his gunbelt as he walked. He was a thickset man and his hair bushed out from under his hat and hid his shirt collar.

Apache Country

'Don't shoot, it's only me,' he said, as he approached Blondie at the entrance; the man relaxed and turned his head back towards the light.

'Any signs?'

The sentry shook his head, and ran his hand over his hair.

'Nary a one. But they's out there, aw right. I kin feel 'em.'

'Where's Carver and Ned?'

'Taken the woman and one o' the wagons and gone to get the guns.'

'Kids, too?'

'On'y way to make 'er do as she's told. Kids are with 'er and her man's back here with us.'

'Hey! I'd forgotten him,' said Bushy Hair. 'I better go and check on him and git 'im a drink.'

Blondie shrugged and laughed. He was rolling a cigarette and concentrating on what he was doing. 'Let 'im wait. He'll come to no harm there. You might water the stock, though. We'll need them horses to move the wagons, after the trade.'

Bushy Hair was more interested in the smoke. 'Borrow me the makins',' he said. 'I ain't had a smoke in a week. I run out.'

Blondie eyed him with a derisive grin.

'Then you shoulda stole some off the pilgrim back there,' he said. 'Or wait till Ned and Jesse come back and try them. Iffen I give you mine, I'll run out, too.'

Bushy Hair's expression was ugly; Japhet could see it in the reflected light from outside.

'One day, Zak, you'll push it just that li'l bit too far an' end up dead,' he said, his voice thick in his throat.

Apache Country

'Wanna make it now?' Blondie laughed. His back was towards Japhet, but the tension in the man was visible. He was standing, legs braced, his hand hovering over the butt of his gun, but he had not yet put down his rifle, which was in his left hand. Bushy Hair would have to drop his rifle, which he held in his right hand, before he could even begin to draw. He had no chance.

He swung and looked out of the entrance, then shouldered past the blond gunman, and started back into the cave.

Japhet realized the man was making for the big cavern and the wagon, and therefore for himself.

Moving as fast as he could in the dark, he backed through the archway and ran along what he hoped was the very middle of the road. Then he realized he was throwing a very faint shadow. Behind him, Bushy Hair was carrying a lantern. With any luck, the light close to his eyes would make it harder for him to see beyond it.

Then Japhet realized he had run past the turning into the big cavern. By the time he had started back, the light had come into sight round the kink, and then disappeared again as Bushy Hair turned into the passage which led to the cavern.

If he watered the stock first, Japhet had time to slip past and sit down with his back against the wagon wheel again. Otherwise, his escape would be obvious, and he was desperately worried that if he was seen to have escaped, it might bring harm to his family.

But Bushy Hair was more desperate for a smoke

than he was to water horses which were not his property and not his concern. He walked past the horse cave and into the big cavern.

Japhet picked up a large stone from the floor, and walked after him as he approached the wagon.

'Hey, pilgrim,' the outlaw called, roughly. 'You got the makin's for a smoke in that wagon o' yours? Hear tell you come West outfitted right fancy. . . .'

His voice trailed off as he rounded the wagon, and saw the cut ropes lying beside the wagon wheel, a wagon wheel bereft of its prisoner.

'What? Hey where'd ya go. . .' he said, and Japhet smashed the rock into his head.

It was a stupendous blow, born of frustrated rage and fear for his family, and it hammered through hat, bushy hair and skull like an egg. Bushy Hair was dead before he hit the floor, and Japhet was armed at last.

Moving as fast as he could, he stripped off gunbelt and holster, and fastened them around his own waist. He pulled the man's body into a sitting position by the wheel, punched his hat into a more or less natural shape, tied the ruined head upright to the spoke of the wheel, and jammed the hat onto it again, as though it had fallen over the man's eyes.

He checked both the Colt .44 and the new Winchester rifle to find them both fully loaded, with the exception of the usual empty chamber under the hammer of the pistol.

Any moment now, blond Zak would wonder where his relief sentinel had gone to and might come looking. Japhet had no illusions: now that he had killed,

Apache Country

there was no chance to return to his policy of wait and watch. No matter how many men were involved in this situation, his best chance to was to carry the attack to them.

Zak would have to go. Preferably, he would go silently, for fear of alerting other gunmen in the caves. But if not silently, then so be it.

Japhet collected the horses, and walked between them as he led them towards the entrance, carrying the lantern in his left hand and the reins in his right.

Also in his right was the loaded and cocked rifle. He held it at waist height and trained to his left. If Zak came within the arc of fire, he would get the blast right in the middle of his body.

Shielded by the horses and carrying a man's life in his hands, Japhet set off to kill for the second time in his life.

ELEVEN

Murphy found the wagon tracks before midday. They had turned off in the trees and crossed the creek about halfway down the big meadow. The Apache horses had followed them as far as the water. Later, one wagon had recrossed the creek, and gone off towards the north where the creek disappeared under the cliffs. The Apaches had followed it.

They had crossed the creek right here, he calculated, because there was some kind of a cave in the cliffs opposite. He could see, through a screen of cottonwoods, sumacs and shrubs on the far bank, that the cliff beetled over the water like a frown, and he reckoned the frown at one place concealed a cave. If it was big enough to conceal two wagons and their teams, it must be considerable. If it was considerable, then the Apache knew about it.

Further to the north, he could see the ruins of a cliff dwelling in one of the huge arched alcoves which was more typical up in the north.

So what happened to the second wagon? It went across the creek, but it didn't come back.

He straightened up, and looked across the creek.

Apache Country

Although he believed a cave to be there, he could not actually see the mouth of it. The base of the cliff was veiled with a growth of velvet ash, and there were cottonwoods with their branches splayed against the cliff face.

He crossed the creek, slipped out of the saddle, took his rifle from the boot, and, walking with great care among the stones, began to follow the line of the cliff face. It was a difficult path, because the broken detritus along the cliff was partly masked with undergrowth, and turned under his foot.

Once, as he passed a natural shelf, a rattlesnake raised its head and gave a warning rattle, and he took a prudent step to one side, out of striking distance.

He was looking at the cave mouth for nearly a minute before he realized what it was. The low archway was at an angle so that from the south, it appeared merely to be an overlapping buttress of the cliff. It was not until he was almost parallel with it that its true nature became obvious, and he froze instantly.

He could hear a movement within the cave, and it turned him into a statue. Caught with his Winchester in his right hand, the muzzle pointing across his body, away from the cave mouth, he would have to step fully into the entrance before he could bring it into play, and that would mean exposing himself to the fire of whoever was waiting. The sounds coming from the cavern puzzled him. He could hear horses walking, then a man's voice.

'Hold it right there,' it said.

Apache Country

Murphy froze, then looked towards the opening. He could see nothing but bare rock.

'Where you takin' them horses?'

Horses? For a wild moment, Murphy stared around him. Then the obvious answer occurred.

There was a mumbled reply.

'You check on that pilgrim? He died yet?' It was followed by a chuckle, then the horses moved restlessly, their shoes grating against the rocks inside the entrance.

'Here, gimme one of them horses, and I'll water him.'

There was a muttered protest, then the sound of a surprised exclamation, and a gun roared, the sound magnified by the cave mouth.

The horses exploded out of the cave, dragging a man who was hanging onto their halters with one hand and a rifle in the other. By the time he had hit the water, his hand had become disentangled from the horses, and they ran out into the meadow, and slowly came to a halt. Then, drawn by the smell of the water, began to make their way back to the creek.

Murphy stepped into the cave and almost measured his length over the body of a blond-haired man who was twisting slowly, hands clamped to his belly, mouth open in silent agony. There was a pistol lying some feet away, cocked but not discharged.

He turned to see the dragged man climbing dizzily to his feet from the creek bed. His clothes were soaked, but he was still clutching the rifle, and he gestured weakly with it at Murphy.

Apache Country

'Mister,' said Murphy 'If your name ain't Japhet, you better get rid o' that Winchester, or I'll kill you.'

He glanced at the twisting, obviously dying man on the cave floor.

'And if his name is Japhet, I'll kill you anyways. One way or another, drop it!'

Japhet stared at him for a long moment, trying to reason with brains which had just been dragged over several yards of broken rock and then dumped in a river. Then he dropped the gun at his feet.

'I'm Japhet Davey,' he croaked, finally. 'Who're you?'

'Name's Murphy,' said a voice from across the creek. 'And that's truly Japhet, Murph. You can let him live. Where's Babs and the children, Japhet?'

Leading both their horses, Rosemary crossed the creek, holding her skirts out of the water. Murphy took his eyes off the dying man to note that she had a well-turned ankle, then looked back at Japhet, who was sitting on the ground with his head in his hands.

The man's expression as he looked at Rosemary was a mixture of relief and despair. 'I don't know where she is,' he said, brokenly. 'I was just goin' off to find her when this guy stopped me. I had to shoot him. Is he dead?'

Murphy looked up from the side of the blond-headed man.

'Sure is. Your bullet hit his belt buckle and druv it straight through his backbone,' he said. 'You could drive a wagon through him, now. Comanchero, name of Zebedee Kovak. They call him Zak. No loss.'

Apache Country

He straightened, looking at Japhet with open admiration.

'Best shot you could've made,' he said. 'You do it a-purpose?'

Japhet shook his head. 'I'm a simple farmer, not a gunman,' he said. 'I knew if I had to shoot him, it had to be right through the middle. He walked in on me, and I just pulled the trigger.'

Rosemary put her arms round Japhet and hugged him while he talked. She was delighted to see the man she regarded as being a part of her family, and it showed. Murphy felt a slight pang of jealousy, and was irritated to recognize it for what it was.

'I was a prisoner here, and they took Babs and the children and went off while I was in the back of the big cave. I don't know where they went.'

Murphy looked out at the meadow. There was no sign of life, and it was just possible that the report, restricted by the cave, had not reached to where the other wagon and the Indians had gone.

'Better take this.' He picked up the revolver from the floor, uncocked it, and tossed it to Japhet, who caught it. He also checked that it was loaded and stuck it down his waist band. He was getting back to normal from his dazed state very quickly, Murphy noted.

'Zak the only one here?' he said. 'What happened to Fuller and Carver?'

Rosemary saw Japhet's puzzled expression, and explained.

'I knew them as Brennan and Darker,' he said. 'They must have gone off with Babs and the chil-

Apache Country

dren. No, there was another man. He's back there with the wagon. Can't we get goin'? Babs'll be expecting me to come for her.'

Murphy had tensed, looking into the gloom. Japhet shook his head. 'He's dead,' he said. 'I left him as a decoy, but he wasn't needed.'

Murphy examined him carefully. 'Good thing we ain't got that many simple farmers in this country,' he said laconically. 'We'd be depopulated in a week or so.' He pointed at the body. 'He didn't walk here,' he said. 'There must be some more horses somewheres. Let's go look.'

They lit the lanterns which were hanging from rough pegs, and walked back into the cave system. With the increased light, and the horse smell, they soon found the stable in which the outlaws kept their horses. There were four stalls, all of them occupied, and four saddles were racked over a rail against the wall. A dim lantern hung on a hook, and water ran through a trough, disappearing into a crack in the wall.

Japhet pointed at two of the horses.

'That's Darker's and that's Brennan's,' he said. 'They must have gone in the wagon.'

'Or had spare horses,' Murphy opined. 'Better get saddled up.'

Japhet threw a blanket over one of the horses and cinched the saddle into place. There were some saddlebags on the rail, too, and Murphy turned them out.

'Clean enough, if it'll fit,' he said, and tossed over a shirt which had been neatly folded into one of them. 'There's pants here, too, if you fit 'em.'

Apache Country

Japhet stripped off the rags of shirt which were left to him after his career through the rocks and the water, and Rosemary winced at the bruises and scrapes revealed.

'You better keep movin',' Murphy advised, 'lessen you stiffen up. You're goin' to need to be limber.'

They rode strung out in a search line, each following a chosen track. Murphy left Rosemary and Japhet to follow the wagon, while he trailed the Apache.

There were about half a dozen of them, he reckoned, though one horse seemed to be travelling light. It was shod, and he recognized the tracks of the army mount, trailed along for its usefulness later. Of the other horses, two were shod.

The riders had spread out, following the wagon tracks but riding off to one side, away from the creek. Possibly they did not trust the easy cover offered by the trees and vegetation along the creek banks. How far they were behind the wagon he could not work out and, of course their motives were unknown.

He glanced every so often over towards Rosemary and Japhet, who were riding in the wagon tracks. Japhet was controlling his urge to rush forward, but it was obviously a strain.

Murphy had come across many immigrant families. The ones who had made it this far were, by definition, the toughest of the bunch, but few of them would have showed such strength of character as these two, faced with the same awful circumstances.

He was filled with admiration towards Japhet,

Apache Country

but he was impressed more and more with Rosemary. In this land, with its merciless heat and hostile terrain, where every plant seemed designed to spike, poison or mutilate, and every creature to bite or sting, most women became understandably distressed and finally defeated.

Rosemary seemed to thrive on it. She had kept pace with him day after day, and he was aware that he had set a gruelling course. When danger threatened, she simply cocked her rifle, and watched his back. She had not complained about the heat, the lack of water or the perpetual threat of Indian attack.

He found himself wondering how well she could cook.

TWELVE

The Apache were waiting behind some rocks across the creek from the cliff dwellings. Murphy left the horses with Rosemary and Japhet behind a stand of cottonwood, and belly crawled through the grass until he could see the point where the wagon had crossed the river.

Even from the cover of the grass and shrubs, Murphy could see the wagon. It was stopped at the foot of a series of hand and foot-holds which, in turn, led to a ladder standing on a ledge, and which led up to the foot of the cave in which the old ruins were standing. Like the ones he had seen further north, they looked like nothing so much as a pile of packing cases stacked on a ledge within a great flaring alcove.

A few of the ladders which looked like those once used to get up and down the outer faces were to be seen, but, since the houses had not been occupied since time immemorial, Murphy would not have trusted the originals.

The comancheros, however, must have replaced

Apache Country

them. He could see Darker letting down long wooden boxes from the top of one of the buildings to Brennan, his rope running through a surprisingly complicated series of blocks and tackle. Even so, he could handle only one box at a time.

Brennan was letting them down to make a pile at his position. He stacked them neatly, criss-crossed like a log fire.

Near him, against the wall of one of the old buildings, Murphy could see blonde hair. Presumably Babs and the children. In the harsh light they were unmoving.

A thousand and more years those buildings had sat there, the Indians claimed, peopled only by rattlesnakes, scorpions and the ghosts of the unquiet dead. They were nothing to do with the Navajo and the Hopi, and the Pima and Papago, who refused to go anywhere near them. He was not sure if the Apache felt the same, but one way or another, they did not use the old abandoned houses.

He had explored Montezuma Castle up near Camp Verde, in detail himself, and he knew that in that ruin at any rate, those buildings huddled against the cliff face had an escape route which ran along the back lower corners of the rooms. All a man had to do was slip along the base at the back, and he would find, usually masked by piles of stone and rubbish, a corridor of entrances he could crawl through.

Of course, scorpions and black widows liked piles of stone and rubbish as well, so it was a good idea to go carefully. Very carefully.

Now, he needed a way to get to the buildings

which did not involve climbing up the cliff face in full view of a dozen Apache and two comancheros.

He needed a way, too, of preventing the selling of the guns.

If it had not been for the woman and the children, he would have simply fired at one side or the other and let them fight it out to their hearts' content. But he could not risk their lives.

He was wriggling back along his own track when the third factor entered into the equation, first as a vibration in the earth and then the sound of hoofs.

No sign of the horses, or Japhet or Rosemary, was to be seen. He turned his attention to the south. A second group of Apache were coming along, following the tracks, and well spread out. Presumably the customers for the rifles. He heard a shout, made tiny by the distance, and looked at the cliff to see Darker gesturing at Brennan. The big man looked round, saw the Apache, and ran back to the building where he appeared to be forcing Babs to her feet. He dragged her to the top of the cliff face, and shouted out to the approaching Indians, gesturing at her. He seemed to be offering her to the Indians, possibly as a part of the deal.

There was a high-pitched yell from the approaching group, and they urged their horses into a canter, to splash into the creek, where they sat looking up at the ruins.

One man, who wore a blue, cavalry-trooper's jacket and had a red and white bandanna round his head, walked forward to the foot of the cliff and started to climb the handholds to the alcove.

Brennan shouted angrily at him and made negative gestures, but the Indian ignored him, and went on climbing.

'I reckon the deal's off,' Murphy told himself silently. 'But they still want the guns. Woman, too, I'd reckon. Were I you, Ned, I'd not be there when he gets to the top o' them steps!'

Evidently, Darker thought the same, and volleyed shouts at his colleague. Brennan abandoned his hostages and ran for the ladder.

By this time, the climbing Indian had finished the hand-and-foothold section of the approach and was making for the foot of the ladder which reached to where Babs, the children and the boxes were stacked.

Murphy was beginning to take up the pressure on the trigger of his rifle when Babs ran back to the wall, apparently to be with her children. Within a second, however, she reappeared with a long pole in her hands.

The Indian was almost at the top of the ladder, and he glanced up and saw the pole lancing down at him, and grabbed at it in an attempt to pull her off the ledge. Instead, she leaned on the pole with all her weight, and then thrust it from her with a shout.

In very slow motion, the ladder parted contact with the wall, and ladder, pole and Indian began their long, slow fall from the high ledge towards the rocks below.

It took quite a long time for him to fall. First the ladder clattered and bounced down the stone, smashing into the pouting surface, and glancing off into the air. Then the Indian in turn, turning slowly head over feet, hit the ledge. Murphy could feel the impact even from the far side of the creek and several hundred yards' distance. Then the body – he could surely not have survived that frightful impact – whirling, fell the rest of the way into the creek.

There was a short, shocked silence, then the canyon rang with angry cries and the bullets began to spatter against the rock.

The Indians at the creek had worked out that while climbing the lower hand-and-footholds, they would be unseen. Anyway, the woman obviously had not got a weapon, so they were in no danger of being picked off. They could certainly get to the first ledge.

Just to be sure, two of them retreated to the far side of the stream and sighted their weapons on the ledge, while their fellows started the climb.

There was a rush of footsteps, and suddenly Rosemary was beside him on one side and Japhet on the other.

Japhet's eyes were straining to see his wife, his rifle pointing towards the climbing Apaches. Murphy pulled down the barrel of the rifle.

'Look,' he warned.

Babs reappeared, pushing a long box in front of her. The Apaches on the ground started shooting, but they were firing upwards at a sharp angle and, though Murphy and his companions could see Babs clearly, the Apache were much closer to the foot of the cliff and could probably only catch glimpses of her from time to time. Their fire was erratic, more designed to keep her back from the edge than to hit her.

She heaved the box to the edge, took a quick peep to make sure she had it lined up right, then vanished behind it. Within a few moments it was obvious she was making a parapet.

Shortly afterwards, there was a puff of smoke from the ledge, followed by a report magnified by the alcove. A puff of stone dust blossomed on the brow of the ledge towards which the climbing Indians were making their way.

The climbing line stopped at once, and the Apache at the far side of the stream started firing in earnest at the boxes. Puffs of smoke and loud reports showed Babs was returning their fire with vigour, and a satisfying accuracy. Water fountained suddenly in the creek, and the warriors with startled yells moved their ground. They could not see her, but she could certainly see them.

All this time, the two comancheros at the top of the buildings were lying low. They had pulled up their ladder, and no sign of hats or heads was to be seen.

From here Murphy could see the warriors stuck on the cliff face quite clearly, and he had a good mental picture of the relative positions of the two sharpshooters this side of the creek. He aimed carefully and picked off the top Apache on the cliff. The warrior dropped his carbine and slid down into the man below him, carrying the two of them away.

Murphy rolled sideways until he was lying between two low rocks, and peered through in the direction of the creek bed. He was just in time to see

Apache Country

a running shape drop out of sight into the scrub. So the Indians were on their way back to investigate.

A bullet whined off a rock close to him. He had been spotted by at least one set of Indians. An Apache jumped into plain sight, aiming straight at him and he worked the action of the Winchester as fast as he could, knowing that he would be too late. But, as he brought it to his shoulder, he distinctly saw a puff of dust rise from the man's shirt, and he disappeared backwards.

The Indians on the cliff face, beset from below and above, were climbing down as fast as they could, swinging from handhold to handhold. Once they were down, the position would be reversed, and Murphy and his companions would be facing all the Apache at once, plus the firepower of the outlaws high on the cliff.

Abandoning concealment, he rose to one knee and fired as fast as he could at the men coming down the cliff. One fell, but the others scrambled down to safety.

Now that he was exposed, the shots started coming his way. Two rifles were firing from the scrub near the creek, which meant the two Apache sharpshooters were on their way to him.

He fired back, a searching couple of shots into the scrub which provoked nothing, then fell into the undergrowth again, and rolled as fast as he could towards the south before jumping up, running a few paces and dropping again. One shot sounded, but he did not know where the bullet went, save that it did not hit him.

Apache Country

*

Up on the cliff, Babs was at a loss as to who was shooting at whom, so she decided that she could hardly lose if she shot at everyone, and proceeded to do so. She scored one hit on a running brown shape out in the scrub, and she could see a man out there who was dressed in dark clothes and had a felt hat hanging over his shoulders. Outlaw or rescuer she could not tell, but to be on the safe side, she left him out of her list of targets.

Her son, Rory, was loading for her, and Meg, her daughter, watching the building above them into which the outlaws had disappeared, with instructions to sing out loud and clear if she saw any movement at all.

The outlaws had drawn up their ladder almost as soon as they had both reached the top, and she had heard nothing since.

Her attention was taken by the sound of racing hoofs and yells, and she peered through one of the gaps in her parapet. A group of Indians was racing away down the canyon to the south, and a second, much smaller group swinging across the open land to the trees at the far side of the valley.

She watched them go until she could see them no longer, and three figures appeared at the foot of the cliff. One was the man in the dark clothes she had seen earlier, and the other two made her heart beat madly.

'Japhet! Rosemary! Up here!' she yelled, taking a fearful glance upwards in case the outlaws were waiting to ambush them.

But there was no sign that they had been there at all.

THIRTEEN

Murphy left Japhet and Rosemary to climb the handholds to the first ledge while he returned to the trees to get their horses. The Apache may have temporarily retired to a distance, but they would be back.

Anyway, he needed the ropes which were on his saddle and the horse Rosemary had been using. He also took his own saddle-bags and blanket, and looped the water skins over his shoulder. It made a load, but when distributed around the three of them, it was tolerable as they climbed to the ledge.

While Babs and Japhet clung to one another and hugged their children, he drew up the rope, and examined the buildings above them.

The higher ladder might have gone, but there were several other routes to the top, and, with the aid of the rope, it would not be difficult to climb. What bothered him was the silence from up there.

He returned to the overjoyed family group, and Babs showed him the remaining rifle boxes, and a case which contained ammunition.

Apache Country

Murphy reckoned there must be twenty-five guns lying there on the ledge, all of the new '73 centre-fire design. Darker had obviously been trying to unload more from their hiding place.

'If he needed the wagons to shift 'em, how'd he get them here in the fust place?' he wondered.

Rosemary gave a gasp, and pointed. Back in the trees, out of range of their guns, there were signs of movement. He saw a pine begin to shiver, and realized the Apache were cutting it down. With the limbs lopped, it would make a rough ladder and with a few good shots lying out there in the rocks, this ledge could become a death-trap. If they were going up the cliff, they had to go now.

'Keep an eye on 'em and tell me if they get close,' he told the family group, and turned to the cliff face. He shucked off his boots and pulled a pair of high-leg desert moccasins out of the saddle-bags, and fastened them on, pulling the laces tight. With his gloves to protect his hands, they would make climbing the stone walls easier.

He was close to the top before the first shot warned him that things were getting urgent. It was followed by a patter of shooting from further away, and he risked a glance downwards.

The family was firing at a group of horsemen who were galloping towards the foot of the cliff. As he watched, they broke apart, one half going to the left and the other to the right.

He was in shadow now. The heat of the stones was far less noticeable through his moccasins and gloves. He must be near the top.

Apache Country

Murphy paused for a moment to find a new handhold and, once again, the shots spattered out below. He got his hand and both feet secure and risked a look over his shoulder.

While he watched, there was another charge. The Apache, yip-yipping wildly, raced towards the wall, then curved away again. This time, two horses ran in towards the cliff, and from above he could see the ragged shape of the lopped pine tree held between them. While the other warriors kept up a brisk fire on the ledge, these two made for the base like sprinters.

He pulled himself over the last parapet, paused to get a gun into his hand, and dropped into the dark interior of the house.

It was empty. The last ladder lay against the wall, with the rope they had used to pull it up still attached He leaned out over the wall and called to the group on the ledge to start their climb, belaying the rope as he did so. He started to try and get the ladder up and over the wall but abandoned the effort when he realized it was beyond his unaided strength. Instead, he propped it against the interior wall and climbed up.

'Send Rosemary up first,' he yelled, leaning over as he did so, and found himself shouting into her face.

'No need to shout, I'm not deaf,' she said crossly.
'Nearly had me off, then.'

'Git in here and help me with this ladder,' he told her. 'We can git the kids and your friend up quicker with the ladder.'

Apache Country

Together, they hitched the ladder over the wall, and dropped it into place. The children came up it like navy top-men, and while Japhet kept up a heavy covering fire, Babs swarmed up with two Winchesters slung across her back.

Rosemary had brought up her own rifle and every one of the family had pockets full of ammunition, but it was not necessary. The room in which they stood was full of packing cases, some of which held rifles and some ammunition.

They leaned over and fired over Japhet's head as he followed them up the ladder. He was only just in time; the first of the Apaches had just gained the ledge, and raised a howl as he realized the group had escaped, and was running towards the foot of the ladder.

Murphy dropped him with a shot, and together, he and Japhet hauled the ladder back up the wall. There was nothing to prevent the Indians following Murphy's climb, of course, or even hauling up their pine-tree ladder, but they would have to do it in the face of heavy fire, and even crossing the ledge was hazardous for them.

Murphy was hit before he had even noticed the second group of Apache further along the ledge. The bullet smacked into the wall beside his ear and ricocheted across his forehead. It opened the skin like a razor.

He heard Rosemary scream, and then Japhet was leaning over the wall, firing as fast as he could lever the action of the rifle.

'Must have had another goddam' pine tree,'

Apache Country

Murphy grunted, trying to push himself upright with arms which were suddenly made of putty.

Babs dropped to her knees beside him, and began to wipe the blood from his head. It felt as though she was rubbing his face with cholla thorns, and he flinched away from her.

'Let me look,' she snapped. 'I need to see if you're bad hurt. Keep still.'

'We start keepin' still right now, and we're like to be still – permanent,' he said grimly. He started to pull the bandanna from his neck to bind the wound, and saw her hitch up her skirt to tear a strip from her petticoat.

'Saw a woman do that up on the Salt one time, with a patrol of horse soldiers tied down by some Navajos,' he said with a grin. 'Time the fourth guy got this arrow through his thigh, she was borderin' on bein' right down interestin',' he said.

Babs dropped the strip of cotton in his lap.

'If you are going to get indecent, you can bandage yourself,' she told him, tartly.

He wrapped the cotton round his head and tied it at the back. It didn't make him feel any better, but at least the blood was no longer running into his eyes.

'Got to git out. We got to git out of here,' he said. His own voice seemed to him to be coming from far away, and Babs looked startled.

'But how?'

He looked around the walls, seeking the exit which must have been used by the fleeing bandits, but could see no way out. Yet there must be one. At least one.

'Them gunmen got out,' he rasped. 'They got out, so we c'n git out. Trust me. Kids!'

Rory looked at him.

'Take a scout round the base o' these here walls,' Murphy said. 'Look behind the boxes. Look for a hole in the rock, a door, anything. Careful you don't come across a rattler or a black widder. Or a scorpion.'

They stared at him with wide eyes. Leaving them poking gingerly around, he turned his attention to the ladder. Rosemary and Japhet were at the top of it, though Rosemary had climbed off and was lying on top of the wall, her feet waving in the air. There was a lull in the shooting, and he took advantage of it to climb the ladder again, and peer over. He felt sick and weak, but at least the details were coming back into focus in their real colours.

Rosemary's rifle went off with a bang, and there was a high-pitched whine of a ricochet from below. It was instantly echoed by another from above and behind them. And another. Bullets shrieked angrily around the ruin.

'I wus wonderin' how long it'd take 'em to work that one out,' Murphy said. 'Took 'em this long ter get into position, I calculate.'

He slid back down the ladder to find the children cowering behind boxes with their mother's arms around them. Every now and again a bullet fired from below spanged through the space. It was only a matter of time before someone was hit, and the deformed, spinning lead would leave a frightful wound.

Apache Country

'Mister!' Rory said suddenly. 'These here boxes got nothin' in 'em! They're empty, look!'

One stack of boxes was made up of packing cases which rocked easily to the touch. One of the ricocheting bullets had passed straight through the whole pile, tearing a growing hole from one side to the other.

'Shift 'em out!' Murphy started pulling the boxes to one side, and found that behind them, there was the looked-for hole in the rocks. The outlaws must have climbed through, then pulled the boxes back into place after them.

'Git in there! Fast!' At least, inside the hole, Babs and her children would be protected from the Apaches' searching fire. It was obviously the way out of the building, though where it led was anybody's guess. Around what seemed to be a natural opening, the old builders had made a proper doorway with trimmed stones, so it had always had some purpose.

He glanced upwards, wondering suddenly exactly how far they were from the mountainside above. The alcove, as he recalled, was more than halfway up the cliff face. Perhaps the doorway led to a secret exit on the plateau above them.

He called Rosemary down from the ladder, and pushed her after the children, then joined Japhet.

'I think they're up there!' Japhet pointed to another of the cave dwellings, further along the cliff face. As he did so, there was a puff of smoke from low down by its side, and another bullet shrieked around the ruin.

Apache Country

'Don't nobody need to tell an Apache a trick twice.' Murphy swore, and fired carefully back at the place where the smoke was still eddying sluggishly around the stones. The report of the rifle made his head spin, and there was a roaring in his ears. There was a fountain of dust and a derisive yell, followed by several shots.

'What d'you mean?' Japhet fired at another sprinting figure, but it had already disappeared before the inevitable spurt of dust showed his attempt was several feet behind the Indian.

'Spaniards caught some Navajo women and children on a ledge over to the Canyon de Chelly, north 'o here. Rolled rocks down on the soldiers when they tried to git up. So the Spanishers sat back and bounced balls off of the overhang. Cut them Navajo up something terrible. Killed the lot of 'em, one way or another.'

By this time the bullets from below were becoming a serious threat, and Rosemary's bellows to "come and get out of the firing line" were becoming more noisy than the Apache, so he sent Japhet back down the ladder, sent a couple more shots into the ruins, and made his way to the hidden entrance.

Murphy pulled the empty boxes out of the way, and instead lined up some full rifle and cartridge crates, leaving himself just enough room to drop down behind them. He made sure the cartridges were directly in front of the entrance. It would not frustrate a real search, but it might slow the Indians down, once they got up here.

Apache Country

He pulled the top crate over his escape hatch as a final gesture, and crawled back down a tunnel which opened behind him.

It was dark down there. Enough light filtered from the entrance to show the rough edges in the walls, but not to show detail.

'Who's got my saddle-bags?' he said, more sharply than he had intended.

'Me.'

He might have known it would be Rosemary

'They's some candles in the bottom of one. Pull 'er out. We need to see.'

A match scraped in the dark, and suddenly he could make out the details.

The tunnel was narrow and low. Murphy could not stand upright, and had to move with his shoulders at an angle. But it had been hollowed out, or at any rate improved, by human hands.

Rosemary was at the far end of the line, and with Japhet, his wife and the children between him and the light, Murphy could only see the sides of the passage.

'Lead on!' He kept his voice down, because by this time the Apache might easily be in the building behind them. Rosemary apparently heard, because the light receded from him and, still bent and twisted sideways, he followed the outlines of the family down the tunnel.

He walked with his ears cocked for sounds behind him, but heard nothing except the shuffle of feet ahead and the occasional exclamation from the children.

Apache Country

Then Rosemary said, 'Hey!' and there was more light. Murphy squeezed past the Daveys and Rosemary, gun in hand, and found himself looking out of a portal. Silvery and eerie, it was illuminated from outside by moonlight, and he leaned forward cautiously to look out.

FOURTEEN

The man who hid behind the name of Darker, and aspired to power, followed Brennan through the tunnel towards the cave by the creek.

He was a bitterly disappointed man. When the chance had come to steal a load of brand new Winchester repeating carbines on their way to the army posts in the Arizona territory, it seemed to him that Fate had put his fortune into his hands.

The withdrawal of the army in the early 1860s had left Arizona Territory wide open, and for the war years, it was left in the hands of a deeply hostile tribe of Chiricahua Apache.

The result was Fort Bowie, the large and growing outpost in Apache Pass.

A wagon-train containing supplies and new guns for the fort had been sent to Bowie. Darker was not interested in the supplies, but he was interested in the guns, and the reason was a secret which he had come across virtually by accident some years before. At the start of the Civil War, troops were withdrawn from Arizona to prosecute the war further east,

Apache Country

destroying over a million dollars' worth of military equipment on their way. This huge depot had been created by a politician who was in sympathy with the Confederacy, and it was his intention that, at the outbreak of war, a Confederate Army should enter Arizona and make use of the supplies. One such force, led by a Captain Sherod Hunter, actually did invade the territory and occupied Tucson. But Hunter had only 100 men and withdrew after a minor skirmish with Union troops.

What had not been revealed was that there had also been a war chest, intended to pay the Confederate expeditionary force, and to support it in its campaign. Hunter and his command were there to rescue that treasure chest for the Confederacy, and he had done so.

He reckoned, however, without the Apache.

On his way back out of the territory to New Mexico and the Confederate Army, he was ambushed while camping at Dragoon Station on the Butterfield Stage road, lost several of his men, and all his stores.

Whether by accident, or out of pure devilment, the Apache carried off with them the chest.

Darker wanted that money with a lust which consumed him. With it, he could be free of the desert, free of lawmen and the Apache, free to pursue his destiny. What he needed was something the Apache wanted even more than Darker wanted gold: the answer was guns.

The Butterfield Road, along which the supplies were coming, went through Apache Pass, only half a

Apache Country

mile from the fort, then carried on to Tucson where soldiers also awaited replacement rifles. On the way, it passed through San Pedro River crossing, where there was a stage station. Darker and his men intercepted the supply weapons, massacred the escort, loaded the rifles onto mules and carried them off southward into the desert and through the Santa Ritas to his chosen hiding place.

He named his price, the Apache agreed to produce the treasure chest, and the deal was struck.

Neither side, of course, trusted the other.

When his mules disappeared from their corral, Darker realized that the Indians were making sure he could not move the guns without their knowledge. They might not be able to find the guns, but hiding ten mules was altogether a different matter.

The Apache probably ate them.

Since the guns and ammunition were hidden in Indian territory, it could be only a matter of time before they were discovered. He had to move them, and quickly, hence his desperate need for wagons.

It had been pure bad luck that the two groups of Apache had turned up when they did. Indians were bound to know about the caves in this high, hidden valley, but he doubted if they had any idea of their extent. Darker himself had not, and he had been shown them by the old miner who said he had been the first to discover them.

Darker, who was born Timothy Devlin in another land, and known and feared as Jesse Carver in this one, lived by one rule: do what you will shall be the whole of the law.

Apache Country

He was intelligent enough to recognize now that his earlier vision of himself as a kind of romantic freebooter was wrong. The life he had chosen was harsher even than that of the people he despised as 'worker ants'. He worked harder than they and often for much less. The contents of the wagons he pillaged were of little value to anybody but their owners. Money was scarce, and savagely protected. Even a successful bank raid was unlikely to raise very large amounts of money.

He was constantly on the run, slept in uncomfortable beds – when he slept in a bed at all – was often hungry and even more often thirsty. He kept company with men as desperate as he, and equally untrustworthy.

The place to carve out his empire, he decided, was among the softer people of the East, and with this gold, he could do it. He had to get the guns back, and he had to find that gold. Once he had his hands on it, there would be no stopping him. Trouble was, he had no idea where the gold was. Neither group of Indians was the one with whom he had negotiated his deal for the guns – and neither was offering any gold. It had been sheer bad luck that they had happened across him.

Following a frightened man, who was now his only ally, Darker pushed on toward power and gold.

FIFTEEN

Murphy stood on the ledge in the dark and looked out over the hidden valley, plated silver in the moonlight, and hung over with stars bright against the velvet blackness.

How long they had been underground he had no idea.

But now he could see the valley in all its beauty. There was water here. The water he had heard back in the cave must be either the source for or a tributary of the creek below. There was ample grazing, and wood to build a cabin and to burn in the cold desert nights.

The thought reminded him that this was one such night.

A sudden, quiet movement at his side, and he felt the warmth of Rosemary's body as she squeezed onto the ledge next to him, and leaned out, arms braced, to look over the ledge and into the valley.

'It's very beautiful, Mr Murphy,' she said quietly. 'Like a painting in black and silver. Like the desert. The desert is even more beautiful by night than during the day, isn't it?'

Apache Country

He was surprised. Most migrants found the desert terrifying and threatening. This woman saw the desert he saw: beautiful, impressive. Dangerous, to be sure. A place to be treated with respect and awe, but also a place of great wonders.

'You are purely right, ma'am,' he said softly. 'One o' the most beautiful valleys I ever did see. And I seen plenty. You folks wait here while I check out this ledge.'

The ledge followed the cliff like an eyebrow, lifting sardonically until it emerged at the top, where it fanned out and became a part of the mountain. Looking along it, he could see further up the valley a point where the edge was broken, and there seemed to be a deep, black arrow pointing at the valley floor. There was an open space dotted with piñon pines, there, and low scrub. It was riven with cracks and scrubbed by the wind and weather.

From here, he reckoned they could return to the valley floor if they wished, and if they could find some horses, they might even salvage the wagons. With as few as two horses, they could all ride out of here in one of the wagon boxes. There was no shortage of water, and the wagon had a butt to carry it.

One way or the other, he had to get them to Tumacacori.

He went back to the cave and told Rosemary what he had found. She awakened the now sleeping Japhet and they explained his plan. Babs, who had been watching their back trail, joined them.

'Not a sound from back there but I swear I could hear water running,' she said. 'There were lots of

Apache Country

other tunnels we passed on the way up here.'

Murphy explained the route along the ledge, and suggested that they all hold onto the rope so that the children would be protected on the journey.

He led them back among the pines, picking up kindling as he went, and they built a small fire in a little depression where he was certain it could not be seen from outside, and they camped for the rest of the night.

Murphy was deathly tired and the clamour in his head was enough to keep him awake for a year, but as soon as he lay down, he slept.

Murphy awakened in a clear, cold dawn with his back warm and snug and his face feeling frosted. His head was wonderfully clear, and every limb creaked when he moved it, but something gave a muted complaint when he moved, and snuggled closer.

Rosemary was clamped against his back, and the children against hers. Behind them, Babs sat with a rifle across her knees and her hair caught back in a pony tail. Japhet was tending a smokeless fire made from dead pine twigs, on which was balanced Murphy's tin cup, and from which steam was coming.

'Just in time for coffee,' he said. He picked up the cup with a bandanna-wrapped hand, and passed it to Rosemary. She sipped and passed it on to Murphy.

'Best get movin',' Murphy said. He pulled himself upright, and settled his hat over his eyes, the thong fastened beneath his chin. He shook out the ropes one by one, and coiled them neatly, picked up his Winchester and wiped the action carefully with the corner of his bandanna.

'Careful, you'll make it dirty,' Rosemary said, and he shot her a glance.

'Can't get nobody to do no laundry these days,' he said. ''Sides, this bandanna's bin through a lot.'

'Most of it muddy,' she agreed. But she shouldered one of the ropes, took up another of the rifles and stood ready to move out. The children were scrubbing at their teeth with a corner of their mother's petticoat, and Babs, holding in mind yesterday's bandage, shot Murphy a warning look when he opened his mouth to comment.

Murphy, who had been shot more warning looks than most in his time, closed his mouth again, and led them along the rim to the fault he had seen from the ledge. It led steeply downwards, covered in loose debris enough to trap an unwary climber, but with the aid of the ropes, they made their way to the valley floor and along the stream to the cavern, moving cautiously, and stopping often to listen.

Gambel's quail were around, and the air was full of their odd, cackling cry, and once while they were making one of their stops, a mule deer came down to the water and drank.

At the cavern, the smell warned them that the bodies were still around. Animals had already been at the one in the mouth of the cave. Rosemary, Babs and the children stayed outside while the men went in.

Apache Country

There were still supplies in the wagon, though the bales had been broken into, and amounts taken. Not enough for the Indians to have been there, for they would surely have taken the lot. But enough, they thought, for two men for a few days. Or one man for a week.

There were fresh tracks coming down from the buttress behind the wagon, and Murphy cautiously searched down the passageway behind it. There was the track of one man coming down through the sandy floor covering, then the same man had gone back and then returned. He had a broken heel on his right boot.

Curious, Murphy took a lantern and followed the passageway. It was clearly water-cut, and the floor was partly sheathed in sand. He followed the tracks which stuck to the main tunnel, until it began to change into a curiously convoluted slot in the rocks.

As he stood there, he heard curious sounds coming up the slot. Whisperings, and occasionally a long-drawn-out moan. It made the hair stand up on the back of his neck, and he returned to the light.

Behind him in the whispering dark, jammed tight in the passageway he hated and feared, Brennan gave another long, whimpering moan and made one more convulsive attempt to free himself. He gave up when the pain from his broken back became intolerable. Below the break, he could feel nothing, and he knew what it meant.

The shots from the gun behind him had been a complete surprise. Normally Brennan trusted nobody and nothing, but his superstitious fear of the darkness had distracted him so much that he had failed to take the elementary precaution of letting Darker lead through the passage.

'Apaches!' Darker shouted, and then the shots had come.

The first shot had broken his spine and, helpless, he slid down into the tightest, narrowest part of the passage, jammed up to his chest so that even the great strength of his arms and shoulders could not free him.

When Darker disappeared, he lay where he was, trying to summon up the strength to lift himself out, but without any real hope.

He pulled the pistol from his holster and laid it by his hand in case the Apaches or Darker came back, and started to find a leverage to drag himself from the prison. It was with incredulity that he heard Darker coming back, and a sudden hope flared in him.

Then the lantern appeared in the cleft, and he called out, 'Jess! Jess! Help me!' Darker's face appeared beside the lamp. He stared down, but Brennan could not read his expression in the deep shadows cast by the lantern.

Then he threw down a duffel bag and a canteen.

'I had to fight off the Injuns,' Darker called. 'I'm goin' to get a rope. Here's some supplies till I come back.'

Brennan heard him go away, and slipped into unconsciousness. Later – a long time later – he was wakened by the sound of steps in the passageway again, and saw the faint glow of an approaching light.

He tried to call out but in his period of unconsciousness, he had slipped further down and his chest was clamped tight by the sides of the cleft, and he managed only a low moan. The steps stopped, and retreated.

He was reminded of the duffel bag, and hoping he could find something to stave off his growing weakness, he fumbled it into position near his face, and opened the laces and put in his questing hand.

The rattlesnake within bit him twice in as many seconds, then slithered out, and fell past his face and into the depths of the cleft. He could hear it sounding its hissing warning down there while the blood roared in his head, and the first wave of nausea rose within him.

He was to take a long time to die because he was a strong man. But the end was inevitable and the rattlesnake had been merciful.

SIXTEEN

Murphy sat in the cave mouth and listened to the approaching hooves. He had his rifle sighted on the trees and almost squeezed off the trigger when he saw the leaves move. But his natural instinct not to fire at something he could not identify made him hesitate and, while he hesitated, his own horse stepped into the sunlight and began to drink from the creek.

It was an unlooked-for blessing, and he caught up the reins, checked the cinch, and mounted.

He left the Daveys and Rosemary to haul the wagon to the creek and lighten its load while he rode his horse up the valley to the scene of yesterday's battle.

On the way he saw the tracks of horses, shod and unshod, which had come back down from the area of the cliff dwellings.

The tracks were quite clear in the dry dirt, and the horses seemed to be carrying roughly equal weights. Either they were all mounted, or the guns and ammunition were on their backs.

Apache Country

Just how his own had managed to escape he realized when he came across the body of an Indian lying face down in the grass. Rivals for the guns had fallen out.

He returned to the cave and they harnessed his horse to the wagon. It was not happy about the arrangement, but tolerated it. With the children and Babs on board, they started for the slot canyon which was the portal.

The men and Rosemary walked down through the canyon. Within the shadowy slot the air was relatively cool, filtering down from the valley behind, but once they were out on the open ground, the heat struck like a hammer.

He regretted the loss of his boots, but there was nothing for it but to carry on. The moccasins were Navajo and strongly made, but they had no heels and he was used to walking with a heel. He smiled to himself at the thought that when he was a boy, any sort of shoes would have been a miracle beyond desire. His first pair of army boots had scoured his heels pitifully, but since the days when he shouldered a musket for the British Army, his feet had never been bare again.

Rosemary made some comment about the cholla, and he turned to warn her of a cholla in front. As he did so, his eyes swept over the landscape, and he found himself looking straight at the face of an Apache.

The Indian was twenty yards away, clearly dead, leaning out from behind a saguaro, his head framed between the fat stem and one of the upward reaching arms. One arm hung at his side, his eyes appar-

Apache Country

ently fastened on the wagon.

Murphy checked the surrounding area for an ambush but could see no signs.

The body was not yet a day old. The Indian had been shot in the back and had fallen across the cactus. The thorns had caught in the cavalry jacket he was wearing and held him up.

The tracks were simple enough to read. The Apache had ridden a horse to this point, a horse with shoes which meant he had acquired it from a white man. He had been shot from ambush, fallen from the horse, and been caught up in the cactus. There were signs in the dust of the horse rearing and plunging, and then it had been caught up by a man wearing boots with a broken heel.

Murphy waved to the Daveys to show he was all right, and back-tracked the booted man to a clump of rocks, off to the south. The man was obligingly heavy, and favoured his right leg, so his trail was not hard to read.

In the rocks, he found where the ambusher had lain up for a while, his gun pointing back the way he had come. Then he had made off on the horse.

One of the comancheros, then, had got away. Murphy wondered what had happened to the other. For some reason he thought of the moans in the cave.

The Daveys caught up with him when he came down from the rocks.

'One of your friends come out of the canyon and got down this way. Now, he's got hisself a horse,' he said, briefly, and they started off again.

Apache Country

*

They rolled up to the old mission at Tumacacori just as the short dusk began to deepen the shadows.

There was firelight reflecting in the loopholes high up in the structure, and he could hear voices and horses stamping and blowing. The tanks in front of the church were full, and there was a bucket standing by the end of the trough someone had erected for livestock.

'Hello, the mission! Man comin' in!' he shouted at the top of his voice.

Up in the old bell tower a shape moved indistinctly. 'Come ahead, but slow,' ordered the sentry. Murphy could hear the click of the rifle action and walked in carrying his Winchester above his head with both hands.

'Murphy?'

'Sure is, Bent. You better learn to stay hid better'n that, or you'll be shakin' hair with Geronimo. I seen you from way back. C'n I put my hands down, now?'

'Yo! Why didn't you say?'

'Wasn't sure who was here. We bin havin' some diffculties. I'll call the party in.'

He turned his head and shouted, and a reply came out of the gathering dark. A minute later he heard the wagon rattle on the stones by the old corral, and Babs and the children came into dim view.

'The horse better come in,' said the sentry. 'They've got ours in the side chapel. Lieutenant's comin' any time, now.'

Apache Country

'Ain't Bassenger here?'

The sentry shook his head.

'Just Sergeant Kowalski, me and Finnegan. Lieutenant sent us out to sweep west, but we didn't find nobody.'

Kowalski was a Pole, a martinet but a good soldier, and even before they got into the mission, Murphy saw him, standing in the shadowed doorway with a rifle in his hand.

'Hello, Murph,' he said. 'Who come in wid you?'

Murphy made the family known, helped Japhet take the horse out of the shafts, and led it to the water. The Daveys and Rosemary unloaded supplies from the wagon and carried them into the mission. Then he left them to explain their story while he went and saw to his horse. It nuzzled his shoulder, glad to be out of the wagon.

'You have a way with horses.' Rosemary was leaning in the doorway from the old church, outlined in the firelight from behind her.

'Should have. I breed 'em.' He hung the harness on a peg someone had driven into the wall.

'I thought you were a scout?'

'That, too. I scout for the cavalry when I can. Times like these, they need all the help they can get. Government took the garrisons away to fight the war and the Apaches run wild for years. Now the war's over and folks need homes. So they come West, and settle. Need protection, Army does what it can, but they're short of men and short on supplies most o' the time.'

He sat down, and she joined him against the wall.

Apache Country

'What is this place?'

'Old mission house,' he said, gesturing. 'In daylight you can see the paintings on the walls. Real bright, vivid. Built by the Spanish fathers. There was an old guy called Kino, a Jesuit, who established a whole line of missions. You say you've bin to San Xavier?'

She nodded, eyes wide in the dark.

'We're not far from there, now. Just to the south. Pimas supported the fathers, there. Apaches and sickness drove 'em out of here. Pimas're pretty much always at war with the Apache.'

They went into the main chapel, and poured coffee. Kowalski hunkered down next to Murphy.

'Tell me about it, Murph.'

Murphy ran swiftly through what he had discovered. The big sergeant stroked his moustache thoughtfully, but did not interrupt.

'You t'ink these Apache got them rifles, now?'

'Ain't nobody else up there,' Murphy confirmed. 'Sure as hell weren't Pimas nor Papago. How they was goin' to pay for them, only them owlhoots know. But they was only one set o' tracks comin' down from the canyon, and only one horse was took. I reckon one of 'em's still up there. I heard somethin' in the cave while we was comin' out. Maybe they fell out, too.'

'An' you reckon it was Jesse Carver?'

'Calls hisself Darker now, but it was Carver right enough, and Ned Fuller with him. Seen 'em in the San Carlos a while back. They was sellin' whisky, then, and runnin' with a bunch who'd been trading

Apache Country

with the Comanche. Army ran 'em out.

'Dunno which of 'em made it but Carver's the one my money's ridin' on. Ned's a vicious killer, but he ain't that bright. If anyone walked away from this deal, it was Carver.'

The sergeant grunted and hefted his carbine, looking at it dubiously.

'They got Winchesters, and all we got is Springfield single shots,' he said unhappily. 'I want dose rifles back. Soon's as the lieutenant gets here, we better go lookin'.'

Murphy knew the lieutenant's first order would be for him to take a message to the Tucson garrison. One way or another, he would not be accompanying the Daveys and Rosemary. They would have to go back with the patrol.

He was surprised at the pang which accompanied the thought. He had grown close to the family, but even more so to Rosemary, a fine, tough woman. Now there, he thought, was a woman to build a country with.

That night, he settled down with his head on his saddle and a blanket wrapped round him. His back was cold.

The dawn however, brought neither Apaches nor cavalry. Kowalski was visibly troubled and Murphy understood his worry.

Geronimo was causing havoc with as few as thirty or so fighting men, but with rifles and ammunition to offer, his ranks would soon be swelled. The thought of more than a hundred Apache so armed

Apache Country

and pushing north to the White Mountains and the Gila made him deeply worried.

Then there was Natche. If he joined with Geronimo, that would make a formidable army. Natche was unpredictable even among his own people, and the warriors who followed him were a really wild bunch.

There were two turkey vultures patrolling the sky over the mission when he took the horse out to the water trough though they seemed aimless. He watered the horse and saddled it, then tethered it at the rail while he collected his rifle and saddle-bags. They were sadly flat, now.

'Where was Bassenger goin'?' he asked Kowalski.

'Comin' down from der other mission at San Xavier,' Kowalski told him. 'You think you can find him?'

'I c'n try. Somebody should warn him. You'll stay here?'

Kowalski nodded.

'Keep an eye on the Daveys and Miss Dodd, huh?' The corners of the sergeant's eyes crinkled. 'I keep a very good eye on Miss Rosie,' he said. 'It vill be a pleasure. Dat is a whole lot of woman, I reckon.'

'I'll be back soon's I can.'

'In your place,' said Kowalski, 'so vould I. All der nice girls love a uniform.'

He emitted a series of short barks, like a seal. Murphy realized as he swung into the saddle that this was the first time he had actually heard Kowalski laugh.

The vultures had disappeared when he looked up.

Apache Country

But there were more of them in the sky to the north. Several, in fact. Circling.

SEVENTEEN

Murphy had not gone very far before he realized he was being followed. Behind him a quail suddenly took to the air when it should have been settling down to wait out the heat of the day. There was dust when his own should have settled.

Careful, he rode on with his rifle held across his knees until a rocky outcrop dense with cactus caused him to curve away to the west. Immediately, he pulled the horse into the rocks, stepped from the saddle onto a high slab, and threw himself flat, the rifle covering the back trail.

He could see the follower now. A hunched figure wrapped in a blanket, sitting on a cavalry horse, rifle resting on its knee.

A tall figure, he realized. And a familiar one.

'You damn fool woman!' he bellowed, as the horse began to skirt the rock pile, and the horse and rider went into an explosion of surprise. Rosemary dropped the rifle and the blanket came unwound as she controlled the briefly bucking animal.

She stayed aboard, though, and the brief loss of

Apache Country

control was just that: very brief. Her language, though, made him raise his eyebrows.

'Call me a fool?' she snapped, her face red from exertion and embarrassment at having been caught off guard. 'It's you who made me drop the gun!'

He jumped down off the rock, and his own horse came to him.

'Suppose I'd been an Apache? He'd have had your hair by now, easy! What the Sam Hill you doin' on my back trail?'

'Watching your back!' she replied. 'Or are you determined to save the world single-handed?.'

'How did you get that horse?'

'I told the sergeant I was taking him out to collect something .'

'So one of them cavalrymen's an infantry file, now? All a'cause you wanted to tag along 'o me? Dammit, woman, this is my business. I bin doin' it all my life. I'm lookin' for Apaches and a cavalry patrol might get their hair lifted, and now I got to waste time takin' you back to the mission!'

'Watch your language in front of a lady!' she snapped, catching him by surprise.

'My language? What about yours? A real lady wouldn't even know them words! They was comin' out o' you like a spring flood!'

'That was *my* language,' she said. 'It's yours we are discussing now. And don't bother arguing about language. Let's get on with it and then we can get back to Tucson. I want to see these horses you reckon you raise.'

Time, precious time, was oozing away while they

argued. If Bassenger was riding into a trap, he needed to be warned right now. He had no time to convoy her back, and he certainly could not leave her.

'All right, dammit, you can come with me. But you stay behind and do what you're told, you hear?'

'Yes, Mr Murphy,' she said, demurely, and dropped in behind him surprisingly easily. It was not until they had gone on another two miles, he realized she had stopped arguing because she got what she wanted.

They came across the Apache a few miles later, as they topped out on one of the ridges which ran from the desert into the mountains.

The land at this point was divided into deep, narrow coves by fingers of rock which ran out from the base of the mountains. Bassenger, he knew, would bring his command along the side of the mountains, where he could reach high ground and survey the next stretch before moving into it.

The drawback to this was that in crossing the long, deep canyons between the rock promontories, he would be exposed to the view of the Apache doing exactly the same thing.

Murphy raised his binoculars.

He swept the desert between the ridges carefully, and found, just below them, the slightest sign of movement. A long survey through narrowed eyes, and the Apache began to come out at him.

He counted three, and had no idea how many more there might be.

They had picked their spot with care and skill. It

Apache Country

was at the entrance to a trail up a defile which left the lower ground and headed for the top of the ridge where Murphy and Rosemary lay on their bellies, a trail which a man riding the switchback would naturally follow.

And out on the flat, dust drifting from their hoofs, the cavalry was naturally aiming for it.

Bassenger had already taken at least one casualty; Murphy could see a body draped over a horse at the back of the column, and there were two more led horses with the soldiers.

The horses were stepping out willingly and the riders were erect and watchful. Bassenger was running a professional patrol.

Murphy counted fifteen riders, including Bassenger himself and the corporal riding in the sergeant's place, one place back and one to the left of his officer. With the three at the mission, that meant Bassenger had lost three from his original twenty-one which Murphy knew was the strength of his command when he started out.

The company was well into the crossing of the desert floor, and they would be within the arms of the waiting ambush within a few minutes. A warning shot would certainly be heard and would alert them to danger, but Murphy hesitated lest it also prompted Bassenger into the obvious course of running for cover in the very rocky defile where death awaited him.

Yet he must do something.

*

Apache Country

Natche lay in the dust, motionless, hair-triggered and waiting. He was a well-satisfied man on the verge of achieving an ambition, and nothing could stop him.

It had taken time to build up his band of warriors, and he had planned it well, first on the San Carlos reservation, where dissatisfaction was not hard to feed. Now, he needed a raid, a military victory over the horse soldiers whom he regarded as bumbling fools, wandering around the lands. In this he was at least partly right. Many of the hardened professional cavalrymen who had kept Arizona Territory under control had been withdrawn to fight the white-man's war, and had never come back.

The new recruits with which their places had been filled were often Eastern boys mounted on horses which had at one time pulled milk wagons. Natche did not know the term, but a European commander would have called them 'mounted infantry'.

They had courage and they were tough, but they had no local knowledge, and they relied on their leaders, whose quality, of course, varied.

Some of those leaders were good, competent soldiers anywhere but the desert South-West.

Some were recently trained officer cadets as eager as Natche to gain a reputation, but without the essential field-craft every Apache learned as soon as he could walk. If they survived, they learned, and became formidable. Some, as in any army in any country, were fools who should never have held a commission.

Apache Country

But some, and Lieutenant Bassenger was one, were hard, experienced professionals who had learned the terrain and, more important, their enemy, and were the equal of any soldiers, anywhere.

Bassenger was well aware he was in great danger down in Apacheria, but he was not aware of the new arms the Indians had acquired. And he was not aware that Natche was in his patrol area.

Natche had gathered around him a band of warriors. One of his recruits had come in with news of the white man who had repeating rifles for sale and, by pure chance, Natche and his band had crossed the tracks of stolen wagons on their way to the hidden valley in the mountains. He had no way of knowing the connection between them and the rifles after which he lusted, of course. He had followed them for the spoils they might yield.

There had been a small band of Jicarilla between him and the guns, but the battle at the cliff dwellings had combined the two bands briefly. When the white men and the white women had disappeared so mysteriously, Natche and his whole band had been consumed with fearful curiosity. The old buildings had an evil reputation, and they had, apparently, lived up to it, consuming the interlopers without a trace.

Natche had personally looked into every one of the cliff dwellings, and found no people there. Even if he had been willing to make a more thorough search, his men were not, and with the disappearance of the whites, the animosity between the

Apache Country

Jicarillas and his men had resurfaced.

So he had gathered all the rifles together and divided the ammunition between his men. The spare horses had been used to carry the surplus rifles, and the heavier cases of bullets, so he had horses, rifles, ammunition in plenty and already growing respect among his followers. The surviving Jicarillas, heavily outnumbered, had been disposed of.

And any moment now, he would also have a military victory over a large force of cavalrymen. More horses, more guns, more booty.

The surplus rifles and the ammunition his band could not conveniently carry with them, he had buried in the hills and carefully concealed their hiding place. Any one of his men could have recovered them, but soon they would have an embarrassment of riches. Even Geronimo had never achieved as much in a single raid.

He cocked the action of his new rifle and watched Bassenger and his men slowly emerge from the wavering heat-haze of the desert, and he rejoiced.

Bassenger wiped his face with his bandanna, and narrowed his eyes as he surveyed the mountain defile ahead of him. It looked innocent enough, but then, so had the little knoll at their night camp, and it had concealed a small party of Chiricahuas.

Now, he had either to ride up the defile and top the ridge, or make a long diversion out into the desert and return. Two of his surviving casualties had arrow wounds, and one had the arrow-head still

Apache Country

buried in his chest. He needed rest and they all needed water, which he could get at Tumacacori.

He needed, too, to gather up his sergeant and the two troopers.

The lieutenant watched his man on point for any sign of alarm. The trooper was experienced, and reliable. If he saw anything at all to make him suspicious he would react, and the company could be deployed.

Bassenger had already automatically selected a shallow bowl which would make a position which could be used as a defence.

But the scout rode on, his horse picking its way daintily, and without alarm, into the jaws of the defile. Although he was unaware of it, the trooper rode within a few feet of Natche, who let him pass to be dealt with by the waiting warriors deeper into the ambush. It was the officer and the bulk of the force he wanted in the jaws of his trap, and it would not be long.

'Lootenant Bassenger! You are riding into an ambush! Take cover, take cover!'

The voice seemed to come out of the mountains themselves. Even Natche, poised to shoot, gave an involuntary start, and the lead trooper saw the movement, and fired automatically at it. He missed, but Natche realized his trap was sprung, its teeth biting on nothing, and came out of the dust with a yell.

The trooper took his first bullet through the leg, and the shot also went into his horse, which reared in pain, throwing him off. As he fell, another Apache

Apache Country

fired into him, and then fired again.

A bullet from the top of the defile nailed one Apache before he even had a chance to jump up, and another burned Natche as he spun to fire at Bassenger.

Then the firing became a fusillade. The troopers broke out of column and went to ground in the slight depression Bassenger had picked, and started a steady fire at the defile. From the Indians' point of view, they had simply disappeared into the desert.

The soldiers' fire did not hit much, but the rain of bullets made the Apache keep their heads down, and the falling fire from above began to pick them off in their hiding place.

Natche went to ground again, then flinched as a bullet whined off the rock by his face. It had come from behind and above, and he signalled for men to mount the defile and silence the marksman up there. He prepared to disperse the cavalry horses, and sent his warriors as skirmishers against the cavalry position both to probe their defences and provide a diversion to keep the troopers' attention while he and another circled to the horses.

At the top of the defile, Murphy and Rosemary kept up a steady, searching fire on the ambushers. Murphy saw an Indian bob up, shoot and run several paces towards him, but as he swung his rifle to pick off the man, he vanished into the ground and instantly, several yards away, a second Apache rose, fired and ran forward.

Rosemary fired and missed. As she did so the first Indian popped up several yards from where he had

Apache Country

gone to earth, and repeated the performance.

They had only a short distance to come, and Murphy was inhibited from moving fast because he could not leave Rosemary.

He said, 'You take the right-hand one, and I'll do this one, ma'am. They move a mite from where they go down before they jump up again.'

As he spoke, Rosemary's Apache suddenly reappeared, by chance directly in front of her sights, and she fired into his chest.

The impact knocked him flat on his back, and there was a cry of rage from further down the defile. So there was a two-wave attack, one behind another.

Murphy's Apache suddenly reappeared right in front of their firing point, running hard, and both fired and missed. Then the warrior was over the rock, swinging the rifle like a war-club.

Murphy ducked, heard the rifle butt crack on the rock, drew his Smith & Wesson, jammed his pistol into the man's stomach and triggered, twice. The big slugs blasted the Indian off the muzzle of the six-shooter, and against the rock.

He could hear Rosemary's rifle banging away, threw himself on his stomach and grabbed for his own long gun. Down the defile, two men were climbing, dodging from rock to rock, always moving in tiny, sprinting dashes, but always getting closer.

'Keep their heads down!' he snapped, hurdled the rock, and ran down the trail, carrying his Winchester at his hip one-handed.

His moccasined feet made little sound, and he was on top of one of the Apache when the man

Apache Country

sprang from hiding, rifle to his shoulder and aiming up the slope at Rosemary's position. He was thrown off balance when Murphy ran headlong into him, and they rolled together in the dust.

The Apache was up first, his rifle knocked to the ground by the impact. A knife flickered in his hand, and Murphy felt a flame of pain run along his rib. He twisted, put his foot against a rock and fired himself into the crouching brown form.

He felt the knife again, caught the wrist and threw the Indian across his hips, falling on him as he was dropped on his back across a boulder.

Murphy felt the man's back break, and his legs go slack, but held onto the wrist with one hand, drawing his own knife with the other, and stabbing home once, twice.

For a moment, they were chest to chest, face to face. Murphy looked into flat, black eyes, above wide cheekbones and a contorted mouth. He could smell the smoky, sweaty smell, the grease from the man's hair.

The Apache was still trying to get the knife into him, but the strength was going out of his arm, and it fell back against the rock.

'You are a great warrior,' Murphy told the slowly fading light in his eyes, 'and I shall tell them of your courage when I see them.'

But he was talking to an empty shell. The man's soul had slipped away, and he was still in the desert, lying on a corpse on top of a hot rock.

He wiped his own knife on the man's shirt, and sheathed it and, as he did so, he was almost knocked

Apache Country

from his feet by Rosemary who had run down the trail to him.

'Get down!' he barked at her. 'There's another of 'em up here!'

Rosemary shook her head. 'He jumped the wrong way out from behind his rock and one of the troopers shot him from down there,' she said, pointing.

Out on the flat, the troopers were emerging from their position, slowly, looking warily around. The horses were being brought up, and he could see Bassenger looking up at him. He waved, and Bassenger waved back.

'Wait there! We'll come to you!' the lieutenant called.

There was a sudden flare of pain along his rib, and he caught his breath and sat down sharply on the rock, next to the dead Indian.

'I don't think it's deep,' Rosemary told him. She was standing over him, head bent, holding the torn shirt open over his rib and probing it with suddenly gentle fingers. The pain was throbbing and sharp at the same time, and he winced again.

'Keep still!' Rosemary reached over his head, shucked off his vest and ripped the shirt apart down the back, ignoring his protests.

'He got you again, just under here,' she said, and another spot burned on his shoulder blade. He remembered the bite of the blade when he had hurled himself from the rock.

Rosemary used the ruins of his shirt to swab down the wound in his back, and he heard her whistle through her teeth.

Apache Country

'Not deep either. His knife must have been blunt,' she said.

'You could'a fooled me, ma'am,' he said, and winced again as her fingers pressed around the wound. 'Nosir! That knife ain't blunt!'

'"Isn't", not "ain't",' she said absently, raising her skirt to rip off a strip of petticoat. 'Hold on tight,' she said, and there was a stabbing pain along his ribs. He gasped, but avoided flinching.

'There you are. Couple of stitches to keep you from falling apart,' she said, tucking away a small rolled bundle into the recesses of her skirt.

'Here come your lieutenant and his men don't you have to salute or something?'

Bassenger was grinning as he came up the trail, leaning down from the horse with one hand on his knee, his teeth very white against his suntan and dust-caked face.

Murphy suddenly realized Bassenger was a very good-looking man, and he glanced sideways to see what effect he was having on Rosemary.

She was looking up at the soldier with large eyes, and she reached up and touched her hair.

'They call it the luck of the Irish! I swear, if you fell down a hole, Murph, you'd come up with nuggets stuck up your. . . er. . . up your Levis,' he amended hastily.

'This here is Lieutenant Bassenger, ma'am,' Murphy said, reluctantly.

'Well, hello, Lieutenant,' said Rosemary. Her eyelashes seemed unnecessarily busy.

'And this is. . .?' Bassenger hadn't taken his eyes

off Rosemary.

'Miss Rosemary Dodd,' Murphy said. There didn't seem to be any hurry on Bassenger's part to thank him for saving the patrol.

'Miss Dodd,' said Bassenger, 'that could not have been you who warned my command and saved my life, could it?'

'Why ... er ... yes it was,' said Rosemary. Her confusion at being asked was pretty and appealing. Murphy thought it nauseating.

'You have a fine voice. Were you trained operatically?' asked Bassenger.

'Not operatically, no, but I have often thought. . . .'

Murphy thought it about time to emit a stifled groan, and put his hand to his recently stitched ribs. It worked, and Rosemary was instantly upon him, all solicitude.

'Mr Murphy! Are you all right? Lieutenant, we must get Mr Murphy back to a hospital as soon as possible!'

Hospital? Not likely. Murphy had seen the post hospital and, what was worse, the food they served there to the sick.

'For a couple of scratches like this? Don't be silly, ma'am. I'll be all right. Just help me get back to my horse, and we c'n all get back to the mission, and collect your family. The lieutenant here can get you all back to Tucson, then.'

'Just where did you get that loud voice o' yours?' Murphy asked, as they rode back to the mission and a deeply relieved and embarrassed Sergeant Kowalski.

Apache Country

'Helped out on a fairground, once,' she said. 'My pa ran a medicine show, and we travelled with the fair. Good folk. I liked it.'

'That Bassenger, he thought you could be an opera singer,' he said.

'No, he thought he could flatter me silly,' she said comfortably. 'I'm not that easy to flatter, Mr Murphy. I thought you would have worked that out, by now. Tell me about these horses of yours. I like horses.'

EIGHTEEN

Natche roused himself from behind the rock, and examined his body. There was a good deal of blood, but no holes, so he knew it could not be his own. His head throbbed, where the trooper had hit him with the butt of the rifle, but the blow had saved his life, for he had fallen senseless between the rock and a yucca base and the soldiers had been in too much of a hurry to make a proper search of the area. They had left the Apache bodies to lie where they had fallen, and two of them had been shot a second time as they lay there. The troopers were not in a forgiving mood.

Natche did not object to this in principle: he understood hatred, and he planned to give the white men plenty more reason to hate him in particular, but he was sorry that the last remnants of his band should have been so thoroughly cleaned up.

He cast around for his men. They were all dead, and the new rifles had been taken, as had the ammunition, and any silver they had been wearing which was admittedly not a lot. A few troopers' wives were going to get some keepsake presents.

Apache Country

He trickled dust onto himself and sang his dead brethren a song of farewell, then he collected his rifle which had fallen under his body, and set off into the mountains. He needed a horse and a drink, and he thought that if he found the water, he would sooner or later find a mount. Horses and travellers came to water. They had to.

The first thing was to get word of the cached repeating rifles to his people, and recruit a new raiding party. Then he could start again and set the farms to flaming once more.

He had long since decided that the struggle to drive the white men out of Apache lands was an old man's tale, never likely to come true. He had killed plenty of white men himself, and more always came. They never seemed to get any fewer, and no matter what he did to his victims, it did not seem to deter others from coming to fill their place.

The roasting of the old man at the Woolgar farm, which had been his work, had been almost perfunctory, a ritual to drain the power from the old man and strengthen the band. He regretted that the woman had been stolen from them by her husband's act. He regretted the young man had evaded them. The old man had to do, and even he had not lasted long.

Now, he fought because it was not in him to do anything else.

He padded on across the desert, heading for a tank he knew which would be at least half full at this time. It was known to very few, and he would be able to lie up there while his head healed. He would

Apache Country

be able to go through the rituals and mysteries which were important to him to fend off evil and strengthen his soul.

He was almost at the tank, when he saw the track of a shod horse. It was recent, and clear and was being ridden.

Instantly, Natche turned back into a warrior. He approached the tank silently and invisibly, the rifle held in both hands, the action cocked and ready to fire.

The tank was low down in the division of two huge slabs of rock which shaded it like a stone tent and kept its contents from evaporating quickly. There was a small area of sand in front of it, and the desert animals frequented it until the water was too low for them to reach.

The tank was deep. It contained a great deal of water and its depth and the shade kept it cold.

He saw the horse first. It was standing on three legs, its hind leg resting, its head down. Since it was not straining for the water, he knew it had already drunk its fill.

The man was still drinking. He knelt at the side of the tank, his left hand reaching over to prop him while he dipped down with the other. Natche could see his boot soles. One of the heels was broken, badly.

Natche, the Apache other Apaches could not trust, slid silent as a tarantula over the rocks, and stepped light as dust onto the little patch of sand. The man was drinking out of his hat, which he was using as a dipper. He must be having to reach far down for the water, because each time he reached, his head and shoulders disappeared into the top of the tank, and Natche could hear his grunt of effort.

There were few animal tracks on the sand and none of them was recent, a sure sign that the tank was well down, because the animals had given up using it for a while. They could not, therefore, reach the water.

Natche stepped behind the bending man, and leaned over his shoulder, slipping his knife under the straining chin for the quick, deep slash which would open jugular and windpipe in one gaping wound.

At the very last moment the man who called himself Darker saw a second head join his in the reflection below him in the surface of the remaining water in the tank. Then the steel bit and the blood gushed over his face.

But a man with his throat cut does not die instantly. Darker had time to make one galvanic effort to rise. He actually managed to straighten his legs and raise his hips. Natche, still leaning over him, was catapulted over the head of his victim and headfirst into the water. He went down like a lance and, because the water was low, he actually reached the depths of the rocky cleft, where the rocks came in together, tight and smooth. His already damaged head hit the bottom of the tank with great force, and he blacked out.

He drowned in less water than is contained in most cattle troughs.

And the blood of his last victim, the man who

Apache Country

aspired to political power, paid for with the lives of the settlers and soldiers of his own country, dripped into the tank and slowly turned the water a carmine red.

After a while, the horse became tired of standing and, made restless by the smell of blood, it turned and walked away into the desert.

FOOTNOTE

Rosemary Murphy walked to the door of the house and looked out over the corrals to the mountains beyond. She did this often at this time of night, remembering when she had first seen this hidden valley suspended in the mountains above the desert, rich with grass and water, the fear and the excitement and the realization, even in those times, of its beauty and its strange, remote charm.

It was spring and the cactus blooms were bright in the dusk, out by the gate where they grew among the eucalyptus trees to feed the hummingbirds. A cool breath of air from the mountains where there was still a cap of snow, flowed down onto the stoop and made it delicious.

'Murph,' she said, 'I can smell that pipe, and the food's gettin' cold. Come in and have your supper. You're settin' a bad example to your grandchildren.'

He stood up from the steps and knocked out his pipe into the flower bed.

'I think that there grulla colt is goin' to be fast,' he said, as he washed his hands in the bowl of water and dried them on the towel she had left for him. He stamped into the room, and joined the family waiting round the long, wide table.

'Ain't surprisin' when you think what his sire was like. Fastest thing on four legs in the whole territory, I reckon.'

'Isn't, not ain't,' she said, setting the serving dishes before him on the table, and the rich satisfied laughter of the family filled the big room and reached even to the ears of the horses in the stable.

It didn't disturb them, though. They were used to it.